Lateral Thinking

by

Dave Schwartz

Christine – Thank you
so much for the use of
your suite for the last few
days. So very kind of you!
Hope this book provides
a few chuckles in return.
Dave & Trish

ISBN-13: 978-1-927915-16-5

Published in 2018 by Chase Enterprises
Site 312 Comp 59 RR#3
Dryden, Ontario, Canada
P9N 4C8

Table of Contents

Acknowledgments

Writing can be a full time obsession. Even though I spend relatively little time in actual writing, and the output in words or completed articles is modest, I spend a great deal of time in la-la land thinking up ideas for on-going or future scribblings. As well, I devote time to watching the news, watching comedy shows, and reading in search of more material.

Therefore, the very first person I must thank for her help in the completion of *Lateral Thinking* is my long-suffering wife, Trish. She has endured years of needing to hit me with a 2 x 4 to get my attention, although she mercifully never did. In addition, she was constantly available to offer ideas and proof-read my scribblings.

My sons, Jeff and Berk, were also hapless victims of my quirky sense of humour and often served as sounding boards for articles that I was thinking about or starting. Thanks, boys.

My grand-daughters, Beth and Emily, have endured my supposedly humorous babblings, almost from birth. I thank them for their tolerance and apologize for any life-long scarring.

Many friends and acquaintances also became the unwitting testing grounds for my goofy ideas. Most still speak to me. They have my gratitude for their help and tolerance.

I owe Jim Mosher, a former editor of the *Lake of the Woods Enterprise,* my gratitude for his encouragement to start writing a humour column.

Also, thanks to Jim Blight, founder and former publisher of the *Enterprise* for his support and his creative wit in the titling of many of my articles. Thanks also to numerous readers who, over the years, have encouraged me and provided many ideas for my scribblings.

Introduction

It was an accident. I didn't mean to do it. I had no aspirations to write a book … and so I didn't. What I did write was a humour column for a dozen years, or so.

It started when I got charged up about 20 years ago regarding a plan by the City of Kenora to put a landfill site one ridge away from a pristine trout lake. The result was a satire piece that was published in the *Lake of the Woods Enterprise.* The editor, Jim Mosher, liked the piece and suggested that I write more articles and came up with the banner *Lateral Thinking.* My choice of banners might have been *Dave's Drivel,* but editorial wisdom prevailed. Over the years I published a plethora (not by actual count) of short articles lampooning whatever seemed to beg for it.

Once the theme was established as lateral thinking, it pretty much obligated me to take a weird perspective on any given topic.

Even though my annual earnings from writing soared into the five figure range (counting the 2 after the decimal point) it was always the interaction with readers that encouraged me to write. People would focus on the hyperbole and point out how I might have taken it to even more ridiculous extremes or they would glom on to some ridiculous comparison and suggest something even more bizarre. Interaction with readers made writing fun.

Some of the pieces in this book will spark flashbacks, referring back to the days when we were still cheerfully and legally chatting away on cell phones and fumigating hapless children with tobacco smoke as we drove. Smoking in workplaces was just starting to come under fire. "Dumps" were generously sprinkled across the landscape and our pockets were still jingling with unwanted pennies. The so-called Common Sense Revolution of the Harris government of Ontario was rife with nonsense and the Conservative Party of Canada was arising from the cold ashes of the Progressive Conservatives and the hot coals of the Reform Party. So much for Conservatives being progressive.

Sometimes situations required poking fun at politicians, and I played favourites, distinguishing between those at the local level and those at the provincial or federal levels. I have the greatest respect and admiration for people who serve on town or municipal councils. These people have, with few exceptions, nothing but the good of their communities in mind. They give up countless hours and sacrifice their personal lives for little remuneration, pension benefits or personal gain. Where local politicians are involved, I wouldn't consider anything beyond gentle humour. Career politicians at higher levels of government, with their fatter pay checks, generous benefits and pensions are, in my mind, fair game for rougher treatment.

Because of its place in the history of my

scribblings, the first piece in this anthology is the first one I ever had published. The remainder of the articles are in random order, reflecting personal whim and chronic disorganization. My computer ate any record of when articles were created, so I couldn't put them in chronological order if I tried. I did include them early in the anthology if they didn't require explanation or background knowledge on the part of the reader.

Sanitary Landfill to Boost Ecotourism

Opponents of the Silver Lake Landfill site should be down in the dumps. Their resistance isn't only pointless but counterproductive. With modifications and a few enhancements to the design, the site can become a world class destination for ecotourists. Thoughtful development won't just solve our solid waste problem but will provide recreational benefits and economic opportunity, as well. Civic leaders from across the continent will pour in to learn how to benefit from landfill sites in their most pristine environments. It's so obvious that I can't understand why we didn't see it sooner. Get WHACKO* out of the way and develop a business plan.

Just add a parking lot to the site and cut a few short hiking and biking trails and we've got it made. Once the trails are in place, tourists and locals alike will be able to stroll a couple hundred meters over the hill from the landfill site and be right on the shore of beautiful Crystal Bay.

If you're a nature freak, you'll have carried your canoe and fishing gear along with you and will enjoy a little trout or muskie fishing. The fear-mongering talk about leachate in the food chain will add incentive to be a true conservationist and release your catch. Your desire to preserve the area's delicate ecology will be satisfied by picking up some of the thousands of plastic bags that will have littered the forest and shoreline during a storm. Fortunately, you'll have brought along your snorkeling equipment to retrieve the ones that sink too far out to be reached by wading. The scuba divers enjoying that deep water paradise can go after the deep ones. The multi-hued bags that get missed, perhaps because they are too high in the trees, will add vibrant colour to nature's splendour. You'll also enjoy the sight and sound of thousands of seagulls and ravens that are there thanks to the magnificent bounty of the dump. Fortunately, they're now adding nutrient to the lake, and it may one day be able to add a beautiful algal bloom to its list of wonders.

A hiking trail in the opposite direction will take you to Morgan Falls, just a little over a kilometre from the machines toiling to bury the newly arrived trash. This spot is beautiful and has long been a favourite with locals wishing to have a peaceful picnic lunch, frolic in the waterfall, commune with nature, and do a little fishing. The roar of the falls will drown out the sound of garbage trucks as they thunder by.

Another branch of the hiking trail will take you to Crystal Falls, just across the bay from the dump. This is a little known local gem—a magical place where the water drops from Crystal Bay, through a beautiful cedar glen, into the Black Sturgeon Lakes in a series of rapids, cascades, and pools.

With delight you will realize that your chance of seeing a bear is greatly enhanced by the attraction of the nearby wildlife feeding station.

Head for the Silver Lake Landfill Nature Preserve where a guided walk will point out all the ways in which a properly managed landfill site can enhance the natural environment.

Unfortunately, opposition to the site is mounting and alternatives may have to be considered. One possible choice would be the Rushing River Provincial Park. It's just as pretty, and the necessary trails, parking lot and other infrastructures are already in place. Of course, we would have to place the garbage one hill back from Rushing River to preserve the water quality.

As concerned citizens we need to be vigilant. This fantastic recreational and economic opportunity may be snatched from us by such meddlers as WHACKO* whose faulty logic leads them to think that we should squander our solid waste resources by recycling them. That's the wave of the future they say.

Help to preserve the past. Make your support for the Silver Lake Landfill site known and insist that your tax dollars spent on studying the site do not go to waste. Pressure on the bureaucrats at the Ministry of the Environment might lead them to approve continued use of the old site. If that happens the economic and environmental bonanza of the Silver lake site will slip away from us, perhaps forever.

*Whacko (Wilderness Heritage and Community Keepers Organization) was an *environmental group whose name resulted from a reference to environmentalists as a bunch of whackos.*

Nostalgia Ain't What it Used to Be

Back when I was a kid, the old-timers used to go on about the good old days, about how good things used to be and how society has gone downhill. Today's old-timers do that also, but they don't seem nearly as good at waxing nostalgic as the old geezers of my youth. Yep, nostalgia was better in the good old days.

I'm writing this on my fourth generation word processor, a G4, as they call it, but I still cherish memories of the economy and simplicity of my old G1.

People sometimes ask if I use a word processor for writing. The answer is "yes." In fact, I had one before I turned four, although software installation didn't start until I was six and my mother could boot me out of the house and off to school to be programmed.

My first word processor was highly effective, affordable and quite simple to fix when problems occurred. It had a handy undo function on the end opposite to the hard drive. It was equally effective as a laptop or a desktop. It was ergonomically designed and did not cause repetitive stress injuries even when I had to make a kilocopy of "I must not doodle in class." When the hard drive crashed or wore out, it could be fixed in a few seconds with a knife. Of course, that first word processor was a pencil.

Peripherals included Windows 55, which was installed behind my desk and overlooked the back yard where the RAM grazed. A hard copy of the spell-checker, known in those days as a dictionary, sat next to the ROM, which was called a reader in those ancient times.

The Macintosh had a bigger chunk of the market back then and I usually kept one on my desk. Just a byte at a time was permitted because a megabyte was considered very rude. Taking a megabyte could precipitate a few megahertz, as spanking was still considered the most reliable programming style.

Back in the good old days, microchips were small potatoes and hanging out on line was reserved for wet clothes. Having your house connected to the web involved eight-legged critters and was considered to be a system failure even though a good web could eliminate many bugs. The millennium bug was no problem back then. Virus protection consisted of not putting the word processor in your mouth.

After a year or so of using the pencil, I got my first upgrade ... a bottle of ink and a pen. This quantum leap in technology offered more permanent data storage but severely compromised the effectiveness of the undo function. A system crash became much more difficult to rectify. It usually meant cleaning spilled ink off the floor.

Times have changed, and now my word processor is a computer program. Problems with it are more difficult to correct, and I recently had to call a techno-nerd to help me out. After a quick test of the computer and a couple of questions, he assured me that the problem was PEBCAK and nothing that a little percussive maintenance wouldn't fix. A little research revealed that PEBCAK is techie talk for "Problem Exists Between Chair and Keyboard." Percussive maintenance is the fine art of whacking the crap out of something to get it to work again. At least it was better than hearing that I had an ID-Ten-T on my system. That one slipped by me until I saw it spelled out as ID10T.

Hi, There!

"My memory is not as sharp as it used to be.
Also, my memory is not as sharp as it used to be."
–Anonymous

If you're anything like me, and I know I am, you've been amazed at the apparent popularity of the name "There."

I've also noticed a lot of people, including total strangers and close friends alike, think that my name is "There." When I meet them on the street, they greet me with "Hi, There." Sometimes it appears they experience a fleeting bout of Old-timer's disease before they remember that I'm "There." Their greeting goes, "Hi ... uh!? ... ? ... ?, There." Later in the conversation, key synapses may fire and they start calling me Dave.

It's hard to believe, but "There" must be an even more common name than Dave. I've noticed tons of other people being addressed as "There." On the other hand, tons aren't as many people as it was before all the super-sizing started. Canadians' gut reaction to larger portion sizes has been to step up to the plate. Super-size fries have given us super-sized thighs, the Big Gulp begat the big gut, and the double double has as much to do with chins as it does with coffee. It all amounts to fewer people per ton.

But I digress.

The people who call me "There" appear to be

18

the ones who often call other people "There." They seem stricken by namenesia, an embarrassing and unpredictable affliction that can prevent people from remembering the names of even close friends and colleagues. There are many techniques to train one's memory so that namenesia doesn't happen, but I keep forgetting them.

It bugs me when I can't remember someone's name, but I understand when they can't remember mine. Our dilemma can be resolved by asking, "What's your name, There?" But most of us are too embarrassed to admit forgetting a friend's name, so we prolong the conversation hoping for the old synapses to fire. If this fails, we will eventually part with, "Bye, Now!" Come to think of it, there seem to be a lot of "Nows" out there.

The real crunch comes if you (There) and the other person (There, also) are deep in conversation, both desperately trying to remember the other's name, when a third person (There) joins you. All three of you realize that introductions are in order. Have fun! I've been there!

Bye, Now!

I Have Aids Now

I got my first hearing aids about a decade ago but gave up on them. They were awful things. When they weren't squealing, they indiscriminately amplified everything, to the extent that the sound of paper being crumpled sounded like a tornado hitting a trailer park and taking a leak caused a sound of machine-gun fire to erupt from the toilet bowl.

The new ones are better, I was told, and I decided to give them a try. After they were fitted, I headed off to school for a day of riot control, also known as supply teaching. It was immediately apparent that the new devices were overly effective. I could have heard a flea fart on the other side of town but none did. The new aids were deluging me with sounds I had forgotten existed. "Welcome back to our noisy world," I was told. By the end of a day in the classroom, I had been driven to distraction by the barrage of sound. I also noticed that I was hearing the entire cacophony through just one ear.

The hearing aids had been fitted incorrectly. The one that was programmed for my left ear, which is as deaf as a post, had been fitted for my right ear, which is only as deaf as a live tree. A quick switch at the aids control centre brought the aids under control.

Hearing aids have made incredible technological progress since the days of grandpa's ear trumpet. They cost anywhere from

$2.00 to over $5,000.00, the priciest being incredibly sophisticated electronic devices, capable of filtering out some sounds and amplifying others. At the other end of the technological spectrum, the cheapest aids consist of a button on the end of a string. You just stick the button in your ear and run the string down to your pocket. The two-dollar aid doesn't work, but when people see it on you, they talk louder.

I also have seeing aids ... a pair of every-step's-an-adventure, where-are-they-when-need-them bifocals. On the brighter side, no chewing aids or walking aids have invaded my life. Yet!

The Art and Wit of Self-Deprecating Humour

The wit makes fun of others, the satirist makes fun of the world, and the humorist makes fun of himself. –James Thurber

A while back I wrote a piece about how I finally got my hearing aids under control. I didn't think it was all that funny but it elicited more compliments (at least two) than any other article I'd written. It's fun when people comment on my articles, even when it's to say they really suck. At least it proves someone actually reads them and that justifies the effort. Without some reader feedback it wouldn't really be worth the time spent.

Anyway, a friend called to comment about the aids article. With three generations of family members present at the supper table they had been reading it aloud, and in his words, killing themselves laughing.

Fortunately, they stopped laughing just in time and lived to tell the tale. How horrible had the end come as a result of laughing their heads off. Ha-ha-ha-ha, Clunk! It's far less tragic if they only laugh until tears run down their legs.

The caller, whom I won't identify in order to preserve his reputation for good taste in reading material, is well read and has a marvelous command of the English language. However, during the conversation I was informed that he particularly enjoyed the self-depreciating nature of the humour. He immediately realized that the word was wrong but caught in the grip of the senior moment he was unable to retrieve the correct word. Although "depreciating" is bang on for my age group, I teased that he actually meant self-defecating. I was dumping of myself. The word he wanted was self-deprecating, of course, but beating up on oneself is such a popular pastime that there are lots of terms for it, including self-flagellation, self-defamation, self-denigration, self-mockery and self-abuse.

Different cultures prefer different types of humour. Wordplay apparently dominates jokes in some countries like Britain and Australia. In North America, unfortunately, making fun of individuals or groups tends to be the most popular form of humour. It's a shame our laughs have to come at the expense of others, but you can poke fun at yourself and still tickle the funny bones of North Americans. After all, if you can't make fun of yourself who can you make fun of? Fortunately, good answers abound: George Bush, Michael Jackson, Doris (a.k.a. Stockwell) Day, and Donald Trump. Even our City Council gives the odd opening, and senior levels of government are masters at it. As Will Rogers pointed out, it's not hard to be funny when you've got the whole government working for you.

The Terminally Uncouth Should Be Obscene and Not Heard

"He has no enemies, but is intensely disliked by his friends." –Oscar Wilde

Such clever insults were apparently more prevalent before eloquence in the English language got boiled down to four-letter words and a wave of the middle finger.

A recent poll found the use of profanity is commonplace. Gee, ya think? We needed a poll for that? A walk down the street could have saved us the cost.

My advice to those who indulge in excessive profanity is to swear off. It makes you sound like an asshole.

Me giving advice about profanity? There's a laugh. About the best advice I've ever been given was to never give advice. It was obviously a waste of good advice. But I digress.

"But I digress" is a useful addition to articles that are running a bit too short. But I digress again.

My apologies, in advance, for not following my own advice. But what's a piece about crude language without an example or two?

If you're anything like me, and I know I am, you're getting sick of the barrage of pointless profanity that pollutes our air. In all of its various forms, the eff word seems to permeate the air, serving as noun, verb, adverb, adjective, and even

24

as a proposition. It's the meat and potatoes of many feeble vocabularies, even forming a whole sentence for wannabe silver-tongued orators. Example: "Effin' effer's effin' effed" to describe someone in big trouble or something that is beyond repair. Some people would be struck speechless if they couldn't curse. The Trailer Park Boys would have no script. Many wish the terminally uncouth would just be obscene and not heard.

Despite being a believer that profanity is the sound of a weak mind trying to express itself, I make the "occasional" slip, multiple slips per day being deemed occasional. Sometimes my lapses are for comic effect and sometimes the result of some calamitous personal misfortune such as burning the toast or spotting some grizzled old geezer and discovering that it's my reflection.

Despite my opinion on crude language, there's one word that, until recently, seemed absolutely essential to describe unsavoury individuals in a nutshell: Asshole! Not a match for the Oscar Wilde quote, but often appropriate. No other word seemed to fill the bill. Until now, that is.

There's a newly coined word that may do the trick. Ignoranus: A person who's an asshole and stupid to boot. But perhaps it takes one to know one.

One of my pet peeves is smoking. It amazes me that, despite all the dangers and the cost, replacement smokers continue to be recruited to the cause as the old ones quit or die off. Despite all efforts to identify the hazards of smoking, young people are still joining the ranks. A few decades ago I started to do a fake smoking promotion schtick with some of my high school classes. That spoof glorified smoking as the true route to personal popularity and a healthy economy but was really aimed at showing how smokers were exploited for corporate profits and how smoking wasn't all that cool.

It's Time to Butt in on Teen Smoking

I'm really tired of watching my tax dollars go up in smoke. Let's face it, we spend a lot on anti-smoking education, but it doesn't work for everyone. We need a better plan.

Some teens are going to smoke anyway, so let's equip them with the skills do it right. There's no excuse for forcing them to learn on the streets. Teach them basics like product selection and lighting up in calm conditions without setting an eyebrow on fire. The learning of fundamentals is too important to be left to chance. After all, poor technique is difficult to correct once it becomes established.

Intermediate instruction could deal with more complex aspects such as choosing an appropriate stance, grip, and drag combination to blend cohesively and project the desired image. Advanced topics could include finer points like lighting up on horseback in a high gale. Special training techniques, such as staring into a smouldering campfire, could condition students to avoid breaking out in tears when smoke gets in their eyes, so they don't destroy the image conveyed by the "tough-guy-in-front-of-the-pool-hall" stance.

Students must also be taught about the contribution they're making to society when they light up. They provide employment for tobacco pickers, truck drivers and store clerks, as well as healthy profits for the tobacco companies and important tax revenue for governments to support our health care system. Later on, the stop-smoking industry and cancer specialists may cash in. Massive unemployment and ballooning deficits will result if smoking is allowed to fizzle out. The smoker's personal health and economic sacrifices pale beside the overall benefit to society. Smoking demands self-sacrifice at the highest level!

There are a few hurdles to overcome in setting up a comprehensive program. Finding qualified teachers may be a problem as few smokers have any formal training. Classroom space would be a burning issue. Fortunately, classes could be held on the streets in front of schools, in conformity with the traditional use of that space. Everything considered, smoking education is a perfect fit for the Common Sense Revolution and should receive the full support of the Harris government. It's important for all of us to encourage our next generation of smokers. Don't just walk by them as they strive for self-improvement. Show interest. Stop and offer encouragement. Compliment them on their inhalation style. Ask to see if they are using the forehand or backhand grip and if they can blow smoke rings. Offer suggestions on how to improve their stance. Recognize their talent and the sacrifice they're making to grease the wheels of the economy in general and help large corporations to remain profitable and pay dividends to shareholders.

We need to be cautious, though. Make learning to smoke a mandatory course and kids may rebel. Regular classes, formal instruction, rigorous standards, homework, high cost of supplies... They may skip out in droves and sneak into the library. Our future could go up in smoke!

The following article was written just before smoking was banned in restaurants and all workplaces and fresh on the heels of the 9-11 terrorist attack. Some workplaces had banned smoking, forcing the truly dedicated to gather in the great outdoors to practice their craft.

Frigid Sinners Could Defend the Nation

I was driving around the other day and spotted a gaggle of smokers huddled (would that be a butthuddle?) outside a public building, sucking in their nicotine fix. A number of names have been suggested for these intrepid souls. They have been referred to by such names as pufferazzi, smoulderados and puffoons in the CBC program *Wanted Words*.

Their gatherings could be called ashfrays, hackpacks and fumicliques. Whatever we call them, the drag queens and puff daddies are a brave and determined bunch, never so alive as when they're killing themselves.

They're forced to practice their craft outdoors because they're no longer allowed to kill others in many workplaces.

The smoulderados are absent outside some workplaces, though. They are blissfully puffing away inside, while their hapless victims fume. To add insult to injury, some workplaces such as restaurants have a non-smoking section, a concept that makes as much sense as a no-peeing section in a swimming pool.

A raging debate is on about whether all workplaces in Ontario should be smoke free. The biggest controversy surrounds watering holes. Booze and smoking go hand in hand, so the thought of a smoke free bar is a real drag to some. I'm all for the workplace smoking ban. I know all about the health arguments, but there's another compelling reason which hasn't yet entered the debate. The world is in a battle against terrorism, and smokers could play a key role.

Who better to stand guard for thee Oh Canada than those who are already stationed at the entrances and rear exits to office building, schools, airports and other workplaces of many kinds? Our bars, pool halls and some other workplaces currently lack such protection. Turf the smokers out and put them in charge of surveillance. Put the nicoteam to work on national security! Add a youth division ... the nicoteens ... for good measure.

Smokers, an overly maligned group, deserve a chance to serve their country and we need them ... outside! They've already proven their bravery by scoffing at the fear-inspiring labels on their packs of killers. It will be good for the smokers, too. Adding purpose to a harmful and wasteful habit should do much for the self-esteem of this pariah group.

Under a smokescreen of budgetary constraints, the federal government has failed to upgrade our ailing military's ability to defend our land. But take heart. They also serve those who only stand and smoke!

Unfortunately, smokers' ranks are thinning due to various health and social pressures. Clearly, the best place to look for new recruits is at our high schools where willing volunteers are taking up the torch. Schools provide their smoking students with suitable training for anti-terrorism surveillance duty by making them smoke outside, but that's as far as the training goes. We need to do better.

Smoke Gets in Your Ayes

The tobacco industry has always been clever in finding ways to make its products appeal to a large segment of the population, but sales may droop now due to Health Canada's depressing revelation that smoking causes impotence. If anything will convince men to butt out, it will be the threat to that critical aspect of manhood.

But every cloud of smoke has a silver lining. The recently discovered side-effect of smoking does have potential value to society. For example, Bill Clinton could have saved himself a lot of trouble and embarrassment by taking up the habit with regular tobacco and actually inhaling for a change. Slick Willie's willie could have been neutered by smoke therapy. He could have saved millions in legal fees by smoking a pack or two a day to limpen his libido. If successful, he would have also spared his fellow Americans and many scandal-weary Canadians hundreds of hours of mind-numbing television irritainment. None of that TV melodrama would have unfolded, had the object of Monica's attention stayed folded. Now that Clinton has been acquitted, he should turn over a new tobacco leaf. Light up, Mr. President, but stay away from those cigars!

Closer to home, on the academic scene, many young males find it too hard to study. Imagine the potential improvement in their academic achievement if the usual distractions didn't arise.

Increasing the impotency-producing ability of cigarettes to make them effective at an earlier age could do a lot more for academic achievement than Harris's contemplated dress code for schools. At any rate, it doesn't seem as if classy threads have done much for achievement and decorum at Queen's Park.

Now that Health Canada has given Viagra the thumbs up for use in our country, we may see some innovative new promotions from the tobacco companies in order to counter the new threat to their industry. The timing is perfect. Free Viagra tablets in every pack of cigarettes! That would certainly raise some heads. Enjoying one pleasure needn't mean foregoing another. It's a marriage made in heaven!

A Practical Strategy for Looking Young

I was headed downtown the other day along one of the most treacherous roadways in North America … Kenora's Railway Street ... when I heard a loud bang and veered, out of control, into the path of oncoming traffic. "Blew a tire," I thought to myself as I struggled to regain control. As I managed to pull over onto the shoulder, I realized that I was on foot and that one of my knee joints had given out. My Fair-Air-Eh (actually an ancient, draughty Mazda) was parked at home.

That is just one more consequence of getting older. Wear and tear is taking its toll. Every minute of sitting seems to produce two of hobbling. Watching me get up to walk after being hunkered down for a few minutes is like viewing a mini-series on evolution. First I struggle along on all fours. Then, hunched over, I lurch forward unsteadily, gradually straightening into a comic, bipedal rendition of Cro-Magnon Man. Finally, I straighten up to walk like a lame Homo Erectus, as stiffened joints start to flex once more. The picture is accompanied by guttural utterances of "Oooh! Aaah...Ooh...AahI" which completes the image of the early development of human speech.

Our culture adores youth, and aging gracefully is seldom considered. We fight like mad. Check out the products and procedures to combat the ravages of time: butt lifts, face lifts, tummy-tucks, liposuction, butt-reductions, lotions, potions and exercise motions. But those stop-gap measures are expensive, bothersome, temporary and many don't work at all. Gravity wins in the end.

Fortunately, there's a cheaper, easier and more reliable way to look young. Just hang around with older folks! As nearly as I can tell, this method will work for all of us until we're too old to find appropriate companions. This technique backfired on me once when I joined a bus tour with about forty seniors. Each of them, it seems, had packed a steamer trunk with about five different outfits for each day of a two-week trip. And, judging by weight, they each had an anvil, axle or spare engine, just in case we had to re-build the bus during the tour. True to the theory, I looked young to them—young enough to lug that baggage up and down hotel stairs a couple times a day. At any rate, I may not have looked younger after the trip, but I sure was fitter after lugging all those suitcases for two weeks.

What goes around comes around, though. I've noticed some younger folks hanging around me lately. I'm not sure if they're using my method, but I sure don't like them making me look old.

Anti-texting Vigilante

I was out for a bicycle ride on a fine summer evening a while back. I was stopped at a red light when a woman crossed the intersection in front of me with a carload of kids. I saw her staring at the cell phone in her lap as she drove, one hand on the wheel and one on the phone, through the intersection. She was (bleep) texting! So I did what any self-respecting, anti-texting-and-driving, raging grandpa, one-person vigilante squad would do. I chased her down on my bike. I lost sight of her for a bit, but in a stroke of luck I caught up with her parked in a nearby residential area.

I interrupted her, still texting, and confirmed that she was the person I was after. A somewhat one-sided discussion ensued about the merits of her texting habit, the danger it posed and the example it was setting for the four or five youngsters in the car (at least they were safer in the protective envelop of the car than they would have been on the street). She was contrite and apologetic and, to her credit, even shushed the prepubescent back seat advisor when he told her to roll up the window, telling him that I was right and that she was getting what she deserved. I then made a big production out of staring intently at her license plate just to make her sweat for a few days as she wondered if the police would be knocking on her door. Perhaps I should have reported her, but I thought she had probably learned her lesson. Besides, I forgot the license number.

I'm especially sensitive to bad driving habits when I'm on the bike. Bad driving practices, and distracted driving is one of the worst, endanger us all but are particularly dangerous for cyclists and pedestrians. In a car you have the crumple zone to protect you in a collision: the bumpers, fenders, hood, trunk and air bags absorb much of the impact. If you have a collision on a bike or on foot, your body is the crumple zone. There are no fender-benders for cyclists and pedestrians. Any collision with a ton or ten of moving metal will probably mean injury or death. So when you're on a bike it's always reassuring to think that drivers have their eyes and minds on the road. Experienced cyclists like to make eye contact with drivers when possible, just to make sure they aren't about to transform us into a hood ornament. Unfortunately, it's hard to make eye contact with someone who's staring, mesmerized, at their phone.

It's not that I don't understand the urgency and importance of constant, immediate communication of critical details such as the age-old query of humanity, "where r u?" or the story of a life event such as, "u shud hav seen the luk on the cop's face when he busted me for texting. lol!" Seriously, what can they be communicating that's so important that it's worth the risk? The grocery list, perhaps?

Strauss's Waltzes Could Perk Up Old-timers' Hockey

What would you think if you were at a band concert and, right at the peak of the performance, a hockey game broke out? It happened to me the other day! Well actually it was the other way around and I wasn't amused.

I long for the good old days when the excitement of hockey and the roar of the crowd were considered adequate entertainment. Now, in our relentless search for more and more stimulation, it is deemed necessary to have blaring music during every play stoppage. Not organ music, skillfully played and matched to the game situation, but canned rock music. My preference to keep the game free of annoying canned music identifies me as an old-timer.

Music, however, would be a great addition to the old-timers' hockey. Soothing music every time the play stops! Great for the blood pressure and digestion! Great for those essential rest breaks! Strauss waltzes or lullabies would best suit the pace. We could have a spectator turn the music on and off as required. Or, since there are no spectators, and no hope of ever having any, the music system could be rigged to a motion sensor to turn the music on when play stops and shut it off when it starts again. A problem could arise if nobody can skate fast enough to activate the motion detector. We could be stuck with a comic rendition of Swan Lake on ice with the dying swans trying in vain to support themselves by leaning on hockey sticks.

The legendary names of hockey are alive among the old boys of winter. The Rocket, however, is not named for his great speed, but for the thunderous emission that accompanies any sudden, intense burst of effort such as tightening a skate. There's another player equally deserving of that revered title, but there's an unwritten rule that you can only have one Rocket in an arena. Nor would calling him Pocket Rocket have done justice the magnitude of his accomplishments, so he had to settle for Boom-Boom. The Grate One is a poor scorer who thinks back-checking is something you do in tick season and that an assist is a device for getting out of the bathtub without falling. His name is derived from his habit of perpetually grating his dentures together in a futile effort to get the Polident to grip.

While the players may be going to seed, the sport continues to blossom. If old-timers' hockey continues to flourish, there could be a serious infrastructure problem. Not arena coffee shops! Availability of ice is of some concern, but coffee shop seating for post-game analysis is a major bottleneck. This is a critical issue. If the players can't get together after the game, who will address the major issues facing mankind?

Athlete of the Weak

The roster of the Wednesday night Wreckreational Hockey League reads like the Who Was of Kenora hockey. Some of the players are still known by nicknames they earned back in their glory daze. Names like Hack, Deke, Rags, Riggs, Turk, Sonny, and Gert resonate in hockey circles throughout the city. And then there's me ... the token Never Was.

Every week the Whites battle it out against the Blues on Frozen Pond. I had a great night a couple of weeks back ... scored five goals for the Whites (and I was on their team!). That's approximately double my normal season total. The real truth of the five goals is that when one of the players on either team wants some amusement, they pass me the puck just to watch me fall down. The first pass somehow bounced off my stick and into the goal. A few more passes and a few more happy accidents later and I was a star! I can say with great sincerity that I owe it all to my teammates.

Now, lots of the other guys, who actually are good hockey players, score five goals on a pretty regular basis and it wouldn't attract any attention. For me to do it was like Eddie the Eagle, the myopic Olympic ski-jumper from Great Britain, winning gold in Olympic ski jumping, or the leader of the Hell's Angels being made Pope.

Talk about being a late bloomer! This performance came close on the heels of the receipt of my first seniors' discount. The ink on my column about that was barely dry when I got my first distinguished mention in a hockey journal. So what if it's a one-page rag with a circulation of 15 that's passed out by hand in a stinky room to a bunch of semi-naked men? So what if it's main purpose is to stretch the truth or even re-invent it? I was lauded, albeit in a tongue-in-cheek fashion, for the five goal performance that enabled the underdog White team of geriatric jocks to prevail over the much-favoured Blue team of liniment-leaguers, who were on a lengthy winning streak.

They say things always happen in threes. To complete the triad, one of my teammates with a particularly active sense of humour nominated me as the local newspaper's athlete of the week, citing the five goal accident. And, being the only nominee this week, I was naturally the best choice. So, I was it! Athlete of the week! It really should have been a nomination to the Hockey Hall of Shame, but perhaps that's next.

I think all of us geriatric jocks deserve to be athletes of the week, because we're out there doing what sports are all about ... getting together for friendly competition and having a good time while staying in shape—even if it's a totally different shape than it would have been a few decades ago.

Idiot's Guide for Dummies

"I went to a bookstore and asked the saleswoman, 'Where's the self-help section?' She said if she told me, it would defeat the purpose." –George Carlin

Call me old-fashioned, or maybe just old, but I still remember when being identified as dim-witted would cause embarrassment. Not anymore! Self-proclaimed ignorance has come into fashion. People walk into stores and openly pay to identify themselves as dummies or complete idiots by buying specially designated books.

It started with a series of books with titles like *High Self-Esteem for Dummies.* As consumers shelled out for such books, it became apparent that there was a huge, untapped market out there. At least one more series catering to self-acknowledged morons has appeared, sporting titles like *Complete Idiot's Guide to Self-Confidence.*

One title that really caught my eye was *Genealogy On-line for Dummies.* It would equip the readers to research the family tree. Perhaps they'll find themselves located on each of two closely-spaced branches of the same tree, or that a couple of generations back their ancestors grew their own fur coats and a few more generations back they were invertebrates with the possibility of revealing the root cause of their idiocy.

Naturally, the title *Sex for Dummies* is also on the shelves. From the publisher's point of view, I can certainly see why. Leaving the conception of future customers to chance would be a shaky marketing plan. But simply ensuring an adequate supply of future dummies to buy books is not enough! They will need money to buy books and the *Complete Idiot's Guide to Financial Planning* is bound to be a best seller.

Even if you think Medicine Hat is a cure for head lice, even if you couldn't pour pee out of a boot with the instructions printed upside down on the heel and even if your spouse has put a sign in the bathroom reading "Warning: Objects in the Mirror are dumber than they appear," there's no cause for concern. There are self-help books out there to help you. Just ask a bookstore clerk where to find the *Consummate Moron's Guide to Self-Improvement,* and you're on your way.

Actually, I find that these books are really thorough and well organized, and I'm hoping to find a copy of *Complete Idiot's Guide to Writing Humour Columns* under the Christmas tree as an anonymous gift from a devoted fan.

Books do make great gifts! They're just one more clever and thoughtful way of saying, "I love you, you big dope!"

Sleepless in Saskatchewan

Camping is nature's way of promoting the motel business. –Dave Barry

Well the days are getting longer, and I'm looking forward to the return of canoeing and camping and their associated blissful discomfort and soothing danger. The thought of camping brings back vivid memories of last summer's car trip to Northern Saskatchewan.

We decided to take a tent along to economize on accommodation. One night we pulled into a campground nice and early, set up the tent, and went for a stroll to enjoy the magnificent beauty of Prince Albert National Park. We returned just before dark to cook some supper. By the time we had cooked and eaten, the mosquitoes had drawn enough blood to operate a surgical unit in a battle zone. Then, just as we prepared to hit the sack, a family pulled in with an old, mufflerless wreck that coughed, wheezed, and backfired its way to a campsite.

Out poured a man, his wife, and four kids, all obviously stricken by Montezuma's revenge. It was hilarious watching them make their frantic runs past our campsite to get to the can. But once it got dark, they were afraid to walk to the biffy because of the reported presence of bears. All night, about a million sleepless hours, their car would start up every few minutes, belching and roaring, and thunder past our tent to deliver its desperate occupants to the can. It would idle loudly for a few minutes while the necessary business was conducted and then roar back with its relieved occupants. Any suspicion that we might be dozing off for a few microseconds appeared to trigger another frantic mission.

Their efforts had finally exhausted them by sunup and we were nicely off into dreamland when a squirrel started to chatter outside the tent. Now, after the of night sleep deprivation we could have slept with a dozen squirrels chattering and playing tag inside the tent, but our trusty, three-legged dog, Tripod, had a big hate on for squirrels. Tripod was in the tent tied by a length of rope that ran through the tent door and was tied to the picnic table outside. When the squirrel sounded the challenge, Tripod ran a couple of quick laps around the tent's centre pole and bolted through the mosquito netting in a chorus of yelps, collapsing the tent and rousing the whole campground in the ruckus.

That's when the cloudburst started.

That was typical of what I've experienced in campgrounds. I've shared campgrounds with warring motorcycle gangs and dysfunctional families whose idea of friendly discussion resembled a battle scene from Saving Private Ryan, as well as heavy metal rock bands in need of a place to practice all night. No doubt there are many fine people frequenting our campgrounds, but the weirdoes always time their visits to coincide with mine. Perhaps they think I'm lonesome.

I'll stick to wilderness camping from now on. I'd rather risk a bear foraging for food in my sleeping bag than endure the antics of the campground set.

Gasoline Prices Are Simply Revolting

Kenora's gasoline prices have sparked a Canadian-style revolution! To date, a committee has been formed to investigate gasoline prices and over a hundred cars have publicly made a point of travelling in protest convoys to Clearwater Bay to fuel up with cheaper gas. Those drastic actions, which must have oil company executives shaking in their boots, were sparked by the perception of high fuel prices in Kenora. There's terror on Bay Street.

The grey-power convoy to Clearwater Bay a while back was well-intentioned, but ill-founded. The price of gas isn't too high in our area! It's simply too low elsewhere. It's even too low here! Consider the evidence. The manner in which we use a commodity is largely dictated by the price.

Anything that's truly expensive in terms of real income will be used sparingly. Energy must be cheap as evidenced by our widespread and extravagant use of it, and the way in which we structure our lives to depend on the use of huge amounts of fuel and electricity.

Since energy used, and pollution emitted by cars, first became a serious issue about thirty years ago, huge improvements have been made to the efficiency of automobiles. Virtually all of those advances have been reversed by the shift from fuel-efficient cars to gas-guzzling sport utility vehicles. If gasoline had actually been expensive, this would not have happened.

If energy does become expensive, people will easily and quickly adapt by adopting lifestyles less dependent on excessive use of it. We'll see more compact communities better suited to public transportation. Expect a trend towards smaller, more energy-efficient homes, located close to where their owners work and socialize. There will probably be more fuel-efficient cars and fewer sports utility vehicles and trucks, more sailboats and canoes and fewer motor boats, more skis and fewer snowmobiles.

People will find ways to enjoy a high quality of life while using much less energy than they presently do.

Our extravagant use of energy has horrendous environmental consequences. These include global warming, air pollution, oil spills and other environmental nightmares. To restore environmental sanity, environmental costs should be included at the fuel pump. If that happens, fuel will be more expensive, but people will use it more wisely and we'll all be richer in the long run.

In spite of all that, I don't like being selectively ripped off by the oil companies, and until our gas prices are comparable to those elsewhere, I'm planning to be in the next protest convoy. I'll be there, but I may be on my bicycle.

What's in a Name?

Car names help to sell cars! They're carefully chosen to portray power, speed, status, sex appeal and freedom.

Cars like Impala, Cougar and even the Rabbit were named after animals that are powerful or swift. It can be a real zoo out there on the road, but you won't find a Turtle, Kitten or Skunk unless you count road kill.

There are also the stellar performers ... those automobiles named after celestial objects. You might drive down the street and see a Meteor collide with a Galaxy as a Comet cruises by. Why are there no Black Holes on the road, except in the pavement? Why no Asteroids? Does it sound too much like hemorrhoids? That wouldn't be a hot seller.

Car names are all about marketing, but some carefully chosen names were marketing failures. What high priced marketing genius chose the name Nova for a car and then tried to market it in Latin America where "va" means go? Think about it...would you buy a Nogo?

In this age of political correctness, why is there no feminist rage about the complete male domination of vehicle names? Jimmy had a vehicle named in his honour. Why isn't a 4x4 Jenny cruising the back roads with a Sidekick? Ford makes the Taurus. That's bull, but it's hard to imagine shiny Cows gracing the showrooms any time soon. There are millions of Rams, but not one Ewe in "Auto Trader." No Lambs, either. How could there be?

Exotic place names like Malibu and Riviera are popular car names. Mundane place names just wouldn't sell. For example, you can't go down to a dealer and buy a shiny new Ear Falls sports coupe.

Names like Zephyr and Toronado blow me away. Other winds like Chinook and Fart never did get chosen. Imagine cruising downtown in your shiny new Dodge Fart! Or try to picture some young stud cruising for chicks in a brand new Monsoon convertible.

Where does road rage figure in all of this? Are car names a factor when drivers lose it? Are drivers of Furys and Chargers more susceptible to violence than those of Accords or Civics? It's kind of hard to imagine the driver of a Sonata trying to silence a Hummer. That might be better left to the Avenger.

Wormageddon: War of the Worms

The lookouts sounded the alarm a few weeks ago. Invasion was imminent. We were to be attacked by forest tent caterpillars. Fearing the worst, we plotted our defence strategy.

As the enemy scouting parties advanced, we tried to negotiate ... by sign language, of course, as the language barrier proved insurmountable. By attaching unscalable (or so we thought) obstacles to the lower trunks of apple trees we indicated they could dine freely on the poplars and birches. All they had to do to co-exist peacefully was spare our fruit trees.

At first it appeared to be working. The invaders munched contentedly on poplar leaves and our fruit trees remained unscathed. The food ran out in the poplars and, unable to scale the apples trees, the double-crossing enemy legions climbed the house and rappelled down. Right into the fruit trees! The air war had started. Operation Dessert Storm was on!

Next came the ground war. Enemy troops advanced by the millions. They attacked and we fought back. We engaged them in hand-to-hand combat, tearing their bodies from the limbs and pitching them in a pail of soapy water. We sprayed them with a supposedly poisonous concoction of boiled rhubarb leaves, only to find out later that the caterpillars had cleaned out a friend's rhubarb patch. We stopped short of all out chemical warfare. The SWAT team, so effective in a previous campaign against mosquitoes, was not used due to fears of collateral damage.

"Nature abhors a vacuum!" This supposed principle of science was drilled into me by an inept science teacher just after the last ice age. After all these years, I finally concluded that she had foreseen Wormageddon and the devastating effectiveness of a shop-vac sucking forest tent caterpillars into a pool of soapy water in its bowels.

On the bright side, I've cancelled my exercise program. Picking caterpillars from the carpet and my shoes and pant legs has provided lots of stretching exercise. Doing the worm-stomper's watusi down the road is burning up calories: long step ... crunch three worms, side step ... nail two more, and so on. Even walking has taken on a new urgency as almost every step around the yard or down the road produces a few more enemy corpses in the War of the Worms. I see a new fitness fad on the horizon.

There must be a sadistic side to my nature, as I've taken rather bizarre pleasure in driving slowly down the road with the radio off and the windows open, listening to the strangely satisfying crunch of caterpillars popping under the tires.

In all, the infestation has been great for Kenora. The lowly caterpillar has given us something to talk about besides the weather and a common enemy other than Harris government.

The Land of the Daylight Moons

Of course, every Canadian has heard of the Land of the Midnight Sun but few are aware that it's also the Land of the Daylight Moons.

A canoe trip in Canada's northern tundra presents a number of problems related to functions usually performed in the privacy and comfort of a specially designed and equipped room. In the Arctic wilderness there are no such amenities, and you might have to hike over the horizon to get a moment's privacy. As for comfort, forget it. There will be no seat ... not even a log to hang out on ... much less one in a secluded shady glen.

This means means squat, but don't confuse the squat with the hunker. People hunker around a campfire and are normally quite chatty. In contrast, they normally seek solitude and are more difficult to engage in conversation when they squat.

On a northern canoe trip, with privacy just over the horizon (or several weeks away if you prefer darkness), modesty becomes a casualty of circumstance. A hike over the horizon might be endured on a once-daily basis, but not for the frequent pit stops. This makes mooning common in the Land of the Midnight Sun.

I haven't seen the movie *Eyes Wide Shut*, but, somehow, I expect that it refers to the type of unfocused gaze that develops when your eyes inadvertently glance toward someone engaged in a purposeful squat. I ended a recent Arctic trip with my eyes locked in a state of discrete aversion ... open but unseeing ... the result of trying to be aware of who's relieving where, without actually bringing any toothless vertical smiles into focus.

The North is deservedly famous for its mosquitoes and black flies, so when you answer nature's call, it's like having your butt sandblasted. Except that every grain of sand not only stings but hangs around for a meal!

Sure...you can reach back and swat at your fuzzy, buzzy derriere but that defence strategy could backfire.

Women stoically endure these difficulties much more frequently than men, but it was the Lord of the Black Flies who came up with a solution. As his drawers came down, on went the Off. One form of relief to facilitate another. The tormentors were held at bay, buzzing with frustration, just inches from what they must have seen as a banquet of giddying proportions.

We soon realized that the idea has commercial possibilities. In an age of highly specialized products, it stands to reason that repellent used for such a limited purpose could be marketed. If a couple ounces of canola oil can be put in a spray can, dubbed PAM and sell for the price of a pail of canola oil, then surely a few grams of DEET in a bottle could be dubbed Spray and Squat or Bunstastic and sold for big bucks.

The name Spray and Squat was quickly

adopted for the new product. It would be equipped with an appropriately shaped applicator to reach awkward areas ... much like Toilet Duck. Advertising slogans could tout Spray and Squat's new, improved, gentle formula for tender areas and make claims like "helps you to get the relief you deserve" or "leaves you smelling sweet and feeling great!"

Canadian Condom Conundrum

In our never-ending search to understand human behaviour there seems to be no limit to what we launch studies about. Every human behaviour, no matter how insignificant or bizarre, must be studied. The latest such example to catch my eye concerns research into the actions and feelings of condom buyers. That's right ... a university professor did an analysis of how condom purchasers act. Your tax dollars at work!

The study indicated such a high degree of embarrassment was suffered by condom buyers that all sorts of weird behaviour resulted! Prospective buyers would slink up and down the store's aisles pretending to be looking at other things. When the coast was clear and they would snatch a package and bury it under other items already in their shopping basket. Some timid shoppers abandoned their "rubbers" before they reached the checkout. Apparently the sexual revolution hasn't sounded the death knell for prudish behaviour.

Rather than risk having a cashier call over the public address system: "Price check on a twelve-pack of lubricated, super-sensitive, receptacle-tipped Ramses at cashier number two," some desperate condophiliacs resort to stealing their prophylactics. Shoplifters of clothing sometimes wear layers of stolen clothing underneath their own clothing. The study didn't reveal if this method is used by condom thieves.

Reading about the study brought back fond memories of my university daze. I once bought a dozen dozen (a gross, eh?) condoms at once when I was a student. That was back during the sexual depression, so I didn't actually need any, but I certainly had hope. (Actually, I did need one to replace the one that had been worn out in the act of creating a prestigious circular imprint in my wallet.) I did manage to negotiate a really great price for my purchase! Volume discounts aren't a new idea. I can still remember the expression on the druggist's face as we negotiated the deal. In my discomfort at the time, I mistook it for a look of disgust, but I now realize that it was probably some combination of awe and envy.

If anyone needs some condoms, I know where you can get them. Bargain prices! If buying condoms makes you uncomfortable, don't worry. We can set up a safe exchange like they do in the spy movies.

To Air is Humane, to Spell is Define

Spelling has been downplayed for some time in our schools. One possible justification is that students now use computers to rite. Perfect spelling is achieved at the push of a button. Or is it?

To illustrate the follicle of that hair-brained notion I have cobbled together a few pairs of graphs containing sum eros that would escape defection by a spell-checker program. The following story, which makes little cents, was the retort. That it would have been an even sorrier tail without the eros is irreverent.

Wishing to remain chased, Martha almost became a none living in a covet. Instead, she went to consult a therapist who specialized in counselling un-attacked women. The rapist persuaded her to join the university orchestra which needed support in the bras section.

Their she met John who had gone to stud a broad as a young man. Upon his return to Canada, he became a faulty member at the university, leeching on stocks and blondes, and laying in the university orchestra.

When they met, it was love at first bite. After an arduous romance, they got marred. The mixed ceremony was conducted be a rabbit in a mask. The ceremony was followed by a grand brawl which was attended by many beaux and bellies. They lied happily ever after.

Later, during an erection, John became our

fiend in Parliament. When the House was in obsession debating a non-continence issue, he went on stress leave to the Virgin Islands. After a weak, he sent Martha an email: "Having great time! Wish you were her!" Later, that comment was the source of much dysentery between them.

Eventually, Martha was overwhelmed by urging from her gentiles to have more organisms. To break the monogamy, she had an affair with a marred man. Shortly after, their house burned down. The cause of the fire was determined to be a crossed wife. The moral of this art tickle is that you should not put too much trust in yore spell-checker.

Although the bill for this story is a pit ants, I'm hoping it wins the Pullet Surprise.

Consumer Paradise Challenges Impulse Shoppers

I went into a small, rural drugstore to buy a newspaper. The headlines were upsetting but, fortunately, the drugstore was also the village liquor store. To prepare myself to read bad news I tossed a crock of rum into the shopping basket and headed for the checkout.

As luck would have it the pharmacist was also the checkout clerk. Anticipating a headache from the bad news combination, I asked about the best remedy. A bottle of Tylenol was added to the purchase.

As I was reaching for my wallet I spotted the giftware at the other side of the checkout. I realized that if the worst case scenario were to occur, a peace offering to the better half would be wise. A hundred bucks changed hands rather than the paltry two bucks for the paper, but I had my newspaper and the confidence that I was fully prepared to read it.

After a story like that (just slightly exaggerated—the part about the newspaper is true. OK, maybe the rum, too) you'll understand what a sucker I am for impulse purchases. That's why I'm ticked off with Canada post.

Until recently, when what a parcel notice arrived in the mail, I would mosey down to the post office, pick up the parcel and go home. That was it. Finished. Now, thanks to cost-cutting measures by Canada post, I have to fetch the parcel from Shopaholics Drug Mart. Their entrance is at one corner of the store and the post office counter is at the opposite corner. To retrieve a parcel, it's necessary to go past display after tempting display with every product deemed necessary to make life perfect. By the time you leave the store you'll have been frog-marched past clever displays of products designed to make you look and smell better, to make your hair shiny and your teeth blinding white.

Just in case you bought enough of the products to make you irresistible, you'll also be paraded by the condoms. Did you have trouble reading the product labels? You'll pass the reading glasses, too. Limping a bit? The canes are en route! Raining outside? Lo, umbrellas! Getting a headache from the pressure to buy stuff? Painkillers are located alongside health food and junk food, fast food and slow food, eye candy and mouth candy. Every display is carefully placed so you have to see it as you make your forced passage through the store. In case the visual stimuli aren't breaking down your resistance, the PA system will come on to advise you of more needs you didn't even know you had.

Chances are you weakened and bought something as you passed through consumer paradise. At the checkout you'll be bombarded by temptation to make a few more unattended purchases before you leave. Those last-minute temptations will include magazines offering the secret route to six pack abs and thunder thighs without exercise, exciting sex tricks to try tonight and details of the peccadilloes of the rich and famous. How could anyone resist? Contracting out your postal services may be fattening the bottom line at Canada Post but it sure can thin my wallet. I'd rather pony up an extra nickel or two per stamp and skip the command performance in shopper paradise.

Keeping Down with the Troddens

I'm a bit of a Red Green kind of a guy. I don't mean that I've converted an old dryer into a sauna or that I live in a house made of duct tape. I'm just always trying to find creative ways to re-use all that old stuff that breeds in my garage and gives birth to more junk when the lights are out.

A couple of years ago I floated an idea that we get a pontoon boat. I figured that, given my do-it-yourself abilities, I'd just whip down to the marina, buy a set of pontoons and build the rest myself. A few hours later, driven off by sticker shock, I was working on a different idea.

These days my canoes spend a lot more time moping about than actually going on trips, so they were bored and eager for something to do. A couple of them were waiting behind the garage for their next exciting trip to the wilderness.

I gave my head a quick scratch, then headed for the lumber yard, returning with some two-by-fours, a few sheets of plywood and an assortment of wood screws. No duct tape. Honest.

A couple of hours later, a seventeen or eighteen-foot pontoon boat (depends on what side you measure) was floating beside our dock. One "pontoon" was an eighteen foot aluminum expedition canoe and the other was a red, seventeen foot, whitewater canoe. To balance out the colour scheme, the deck was painted green.

Inside one of the canoes, underneath the deck, I put a couple of huge truck batteries, also harvested from the back yard salvage. Mounted on what we arbitrarily designated the stern of the rig was an electric trolling motor. Atop the deck was an assortment of lawn chairs, a wooden swim ladder and a cooler of refreshments.

Some refreshments and a short cruise led us to the conclusion that we probably looked like an aquatic version of the Beverly Hillbillies. The rig was dubbed "The Clampett."

The canoes are much happier now, bobbing cheerfully under their shared load and always ready for their next outing. Moreover, whenever one of them wants to go on a canoe trip, its side of the Clampett's platform is hoisted onto the dock and the eager canoe is slipped out, free of its mundane duties, to go on a trip or play in the rapids.

Apart from giving people something to laugh at, the Clampett takes us and our friends on relaxing evening cruises on Laurenson Lake/Creek and serves as a swimming platform. The big batteries even give us the range to silently haul groceries from Safeway, a unique Kenora opportunity.

With the appetite for the good life driving many into bankruptcy, it's good to know that a little innovation can save big bucks. But style icons like Paris Hilton are not yet cruising around on Clampetts.

There's something absurdly satisfying about using a contraption like the Clampett. Maybe it's reverse snobbery ... a kind of one-downmanship.

We've got an uglier boat than you have. Instead of keeping up with the Joneses, some folks enjoy keeping down with the Troddens.

Interested? Plans to build your own Clampett Cruiser are available at www.plans? yougottabekidding.justslaponetogether.com.

Just Plain Nonscents

Acting on some very pointed advice the other day, I went shopping for personal deodorant. After I had flummoxed unsuccessfully around the store for a while, a clerk finally offered to help.

"Roll on ball type?" she queried. "No, it's for underarms," I responded.

She directed to a display, where I encountered a bewildering assortment of options. Most of the products were scented. Scented deodorant! What a great oxymoron! Put it on the list with jumbo shrimp, teen logic and military intelligence.

I was looking for unscented stuff. If it's not socially acceptable to smell like me, I'd rather not smell at all. However, the things that I don't want to smell like dominate the labels of deodorants. Take, for example, sport scent. Sport scent, in my mind, would include the stench of locker rooms, rodeo arenas, filleting sheds, and hockey equipment bags.

Perhaps the product has a different odour than the name suggests, but I wouldn't want to take the chance. Imagine walking into a room and having people wrinkle their noses while looking around to see who's filleting a Northern pike or airing out their old tennis shoes.

Brut is an old standby fragrance that I rejected immediately. Visualize a brute. Once you've got the image in mind, try to imagine what he smells like. Who wants that aroma wafting from their body at high tea?

Musk is another traditional man-smell with a prominent place on the shelves. Musk oxen and muskrats are so-named because of their pungent odour. Thanks, but no, thanks! My dog rolls in rotted fish every chance he gets and I fear that musk might bring me the same degree of popularity that it gets him.

Baby powder scent was a no-brainer. It's the perfect choice for a guy swaddled in a fresh new Depends, but I didn't want to give the impression that my diaper had just been changed, or, worse yet, that it hadn't. On with the search!

Aha! Morning breeze! It seemed like the best choice until I thought about it a little more carefully. Unless he is sleeping under the stars, the first breeze of the day experienced by a man is apt to be a rude and sonorous zephyr. The scent of those is to be escaped, rather than slathered on the body to be shared with the rest of humanity. There'd be a big stink about that.

Poultrygeist Haunts Local Club

People need a sense of belonging and many satisfy this need by joining clubs. I belong to one such club, and every time I go to the clubhouse there are many other members to be found. There's also a real sense of common purpose—shopping for food and other grocery items like motor oil and kitty litter. Granted, membership isn't exclusive. If you prefer lower prices than non-members would pay, and can remember either your name or your phone number, you're in.

There are no outward symbols of membership. No gang colours and no club jackets proclaiming special membership status like "Air Miles Ace," "Shopping Mom," "Bargain Coach" or "Most Valuable Coupon Clipper."

When I walked into the clubroom the other day, I was shocked to find that everything was rearranged. Why wasn't I consulted? I'm a member of the Safeway Club, for Pete's sake! Talk to me! Ask my opinion!

Just when I finally knew where to find stuff, Safeway moved everything. Suddenly I didn't know snuff from canola, couldn't find my artichokes in bright light with both hands. It wasn't just me. Other shoppers flummoxed helplessly around the store searching for stuff and looking as confused as a starving child given a piece of wax fruit. Frustration and anger were also evident on their faces as they plodded up and down the aisles, vainly searching high and low to score those elusive bonus AirMiles.

"Poultrygeist*! It's been up to mischief again," was my next reaction. The most common theory about poultrygeist is that it is the spirit of a spit-roasted chicken (doesn't that sound delicious?).

The confusion was actually the handiwork of the marketing gurus. Marketing strategy ... Move everything in the place. Force customers to search every corner of the store. Put the leeks where the peas used to be. Make customers look on every shelf to find products. They'll buy things they never intended to buy, spend money they had no intention of parting with. Customers get mad, but are lured back with loss-leaders and bonus Air Miles.

Shoppers were grumpy, starved and exhausted after pushing heavily-laden carts up and down the aisles desperately seeking to complete their mission. Despite the crisis, international aid agencies were absent, although a couple emergency feeding stations were set up at strategic locations in the store to serve tidbits of fried sausage and gourmet cheese. These were staffed by chatty ladies, all too eager to expound on the merits of the products they were serving, dispelling the notion that the food was served for purely humanitarian reasons.

It's not all bad, though. Kind of puts us back in touch with the hunter in our ancient hunter-gatherer roots.

Dreamcatchers: A Nightmare in Waiting

The popularity of hanging dreamcatchers from the rear view mirrors of cars and trucks puzzles me. Alarms me, too. Dreamcatchers are supposed to protect people from bad dreams while they sleep, while allowing the good dreams to pass through.

If you're anything like me, and I know I am, you'd prefer that drivers not have dreams behind the wheel. I hope the magical powers of dreamcatchers can't keep up with a speeding car. Call me a stick in the mud, but sweet dreams for sleeping drivers didn't make my wish list. Bad dreams should be allowed to awaken the dozer before a real nightmare occurs

According to researchers, we Canucks are a pretty sleepy bunch. Many of us are sleep deprived and many admit to having nodded off behind the wheel. Plenty of accidents are attributed to drivers falling asleep at the wheel. Scary stuff.

Sleep deprivation affects more than drivers. About two-thirds of Canadian workers admit to sleepiness interfering with their work. The cost of workplace drowsiness to Canadian employers is estimated to be about two billion dollars annually in lost productivity and accidents.

Waking up to the problem, one Canadian company has furnished special rooms with couches, reclining chairs, and alarm clocks. Employees on long shifts are permitted to doze off for fifteen minutes with the company's blessing.

Other companies are developing similar schemes that permit workers to get fired up for on-the-job naps, instead of just fired. However, there's still a stigma attached to sleeping on the job. Because of this, providing a place for employees to nap is usually an undercover operation. Sleeping facilities are disguised by clever names like "alertness recovery room." A couple of personal suggestions are "drowsiness reversal modules" and "proactive perceptiveness enhancement chamber." Unfortunately, the less obfuscating "rest room" has already been claimed by another serious threat to modern production efficiency. Government ministries could be consulted to provide a full range of suitably mystifying terminology.

The mantra in business these days is "leaner and meaner." Workplace naps, however, are actually a recycled old idea from a kinder and fatter era. Back in the fifties, my grandfather's small-town general store had a back room with a couch. Grandpa freely and openly engaged in "alertness recovery therapy," but lacking a penchant for government-style jargon, he was just having a snooze.

It's hard to imagine a simple nap in the competitive environment of the modern workplace. Regular naps will have to be replaced by power naps. Power naps fit the concept of a competitive environment very nicely.

Simply nodding off or snoozing doesn't. Picture it now! A highly competitive executive at the peak of his career is flexing powerful eyelid muscles, resolving to out-rest the competition and snore them into submission. Picture training seminars with teams of employees attending lectures by renowned nap gurus and psyching themselves up to rest faster and more effectively than the opposition. This would be competitive relaxation at its best! Dream on!

Choosing Sides

If you drive on the right side of the road in many countries, you will be on the wrong side. To be on the right side, you must drive on the left side. The solution is to drive on the correct side, whichever that happens to be.

The reasons for the confusion are historical, going all the way back to the knights of yore, wherever that was. In an early form of road rage, medieval knights, mounted on horseback, made their hostile gestures with swords and lances. Most preferred to do battle with their right hand. To do so, they had to pass to the left of their enemy. Thus originated the British tradition of driving on the "other" side of the road ... a practice still adhered to in many countries.

Driving on the right in many other countries also originated for practical reasons. In the United States and France, teamsters began hauling farm products in big wagons pulled by several pairs of horses. Horses, apparently, were more enthusiastic about their duties if they were flogged when more effort was required. The drivers sat on the left rear horse so they could keep their right arms free to whip the team. Then, as now, most people did their flogging right-handed. To get the best view of the road other traffic teamsters would keep to the right side of the road, a practice that eventually transferred to motor traffic.

In England they used smaller wagons and the

drivers sat on a seat mounted on the wagon. They usually sat on the right side of the seat so their whips wouldn't hang up on the load behind them when they flogged the horses. To see well they had to keep to the left of the roadway. The English continued to drive on the left after the advent of the automobile.

Driving on the right seems to provide an advantage for in modern hostilities, now carried out on multi-lane highways or busy streets. The predominant modern gesture of hostility is the upturned middle finger of a clenched fist. Due to high speeds or heavy traffic, the gesture would be best performed with the right hand controlling the car. Sitting in the left side of the car allows the offensive digit to be extended through the driver's window for optimum clarity of communication.

When neighbouring jurisdictions drive on opposite sides it can present opportunities for (mis)adventure. For example, New Brunswick switched from left to right in 1922 and Nova scotia was dominated by leftist sentiments for another four months. Drivers crossing the border had to remember to switch. Apparently many didn't and mishaps were frequent, even with the low traffic of that era.

At that time carts drawn by oxen were still very common on the roads. Like many drivers, oxen are notoriously slow-witted and many had to be replaced with new ones trained to keep to the right. The price of beef dropped like a stone when displaced oxen were sent to slaughter and flooded the beef market. Lunenburg County still remembers 1923 as The Year of Free Beef.

Because we are such creatures of habit, driving on the left while we were on a road trip "down under" presented more challenges than I expected. For example, I would approach the car and slide nonchalantly into the driver's seat...only to discover that the controls had been stolen. Closer inspection always revealed that the controls were still there ... on the other side of the car.

The turn signal and windshield wiper controls were reversed. Pulling away from the curb, I would have the car quickly in motion, windshield wipers waving wildly to signal the turn into traffic. Rain, on the other hand, prompted activation of the turn signals, which did little to improve visibility. Fortunately, the orientation of the foot pedals was the same as here...clutch on the left, brake and accelerator on the right.

Good thing! Tramping on the gas pedal in an effort to stop is not particularly effective.

The gear shift lever is on the "other side" and an absent-minded creature of habit could find himself dropping the seat into full recline in an attempt to shift gears, or shifting into reverse instead of rolling down the window.

Stories abound about tourists who have met an untimely end on New Zealand's narrow, winding roads. When danger looms ahead, many tourists, accustomed to driving on the right, instinctively head for the right shoulder of the road. That's the left shoulder for oncoming Kiwis. Because they are also creatures of habit, that's where they head when danger looms ahead. It can be wonderful when tourists get to meet the locals. But not always!

Driven by Distraction

In a perfect world driving schools would be keeping up with the increasing complexity of today's driving conditions, but I see alarming signs that they aren't. I watch the Young Drivers training car with its precious cargo of young drivers. Their eager young minds are intent on the task, their eyes are riveted to the road, which sounds quite painful when you actually think about it. They have both hands on the wheel as they roll along well below the speed limit. I can't help but think that this is a fantastic beginner's course. Great job on the basics!

But what about the real world? How are drivers learning the much more demanding skills that are displayed daily on our roads? For example, one driver I spotted recently had both hands busily engaged in personal grooming and her eyes focused on the mirror as she guided the car with her knee. Who taught her how to do that? Another driver was dialing his cell phone while steering with his elbow and ogling girls on the street. Was he properly trained to do that? This is driving in the real world. Time pressures dictate that some drivers simply can't afford to do just one thing at a time.

There seem to be no limits on the creativity displayed by drivers in finding activities to alleviate the long periods of boredom that separate the moments of terror caused by inattention. Does driver education equip drivers to perform these complex, advanced techniques, or is it being left to chance? If drivers aren't properly trained, they may be putting themselves and others at risk.

Statistics indicate that cell phone users have a higher accident rate than intoxicated drivers. This is evidence that they haven't enrolled in cell phone immersion. How can we feel safe on the roads if there's no system in place to ensure that cell phone users are properly qualified?

Some countries have gone to the extreme and banned the use of hand-held cell phones while driving. That seems far too drastic. An enhancement of the present graduated license system could be the answer. The usual entry level driver's test could determine basic competence and after a couple of years of experience, an advanced test could evaluate more sophisticated skills such as recovering from a skid with a thermos of steaming hot coffee spilled in your lap or high-speed collision avoidance maneuvers while spanking the dog for getting his head stuck under the brake pedal.

Drivers deemed to have inadequate performance in these complex situations wouldn't graduate to the more advanced license and would be restricted to paying attention while driving. This would be a severe restriction on the individual's freedom of the open road, but it's not possible to take safety too seriously.

Family Day

Twenty years ago, Alberta introduced Family Day and created a long weekend in mid-February. Getting a break in the long stretch between New Year's and Easter to do anything that isn't work related is a great idea that caught like wildfire and after a mere twenty years it has arrived in Ontario.

When I saw that the recreation centre was to be closed on our first ever Family Day, I thought that perhaps April Fools' day had arrived early.

Unfortunately, it was no prank and the City's number one destination for families really was closed for the day. Your tax dollars at rest! Since it's a watered down excuse for Family Day we should have a locally appropriate name. How about calling it Lock-the-kids-out Day, Do-something-else-day, Catch-up on-your-sleep-day or Clean-up-the-house-day. Or, since the swimming pool is closed, you could celebrate Take-the-kids-to the-poolroom-day.

The possibilities for more appropriate names are limited only by your imagination. It could be Can't-take-Junior-to-the-rink-so-he-can-play-Nintendo-and-get-fatter-day. Or, given that the lovely indoor walking track is closed, why not make it Take-Granny-scaling-the-downtown-snowbanks-day.

Besides, when you think about it every day should be Family Day. Designating just one day as Family Day could be license for some to cop out for the other 364 days ... with a bonus day off every leap year.

Perhaps a delegation to Council on the desirability of opening the pool, rinks, libraries, the walking track, and the senior's centre on Family Day and some other civic holidays would get results. A barrage of letters coupled with a petition, numerous phone calls, editorials and public demonstrations might do the trick.

Note: Kenora's recreation centre has been open every Family Day since that initial debacle sparked the above letter and a lot of other citizen feedback to Council.

Halting the Ravages of Time

"Time may be a great healer but it's a lousy beautician" –T. J. Park

Unlike previous generations, many baby boomers have stuck with athletics. They're trying to stave off the ravages of time and maintain the illusion of youth by staying fit. Exercise has kept many of them acting, looking and feeling younger. Thanks to their efforts, forty became the new thirty. Later, fifty was proclaimed the new forty. Now, sixty is becoming the new fifty. Those weak-end warriors are staying fit, determined to stay young forever or die trying.

There are other allies in the battle against the ticking clock. Long before boomers and the fitness kick entered the scene, Mother Nature had her own method of reducing the appearance of ageing. Failing eyes are nature's way of preventing us from seeing the wrinkles and imperfections when we get up close to each other. Now botox can take out the wrinkles and is a new ally in the battle.

But there are telltale signs of ageing that can't be helped by botox, bad vision or more exercise. Desperate boomers trying to outrun the ravages of time often develop tendinitis, bursitis, arthritis and assorted other aches and pains. Together these afflictions may be called boomeritis or fix-me-itis. Fitness obsessed boomers are earning their reputation as Generation Ouch.

At the edge of the fitness craze are the extreme athletes who push the boundaries of human endurance. For them, twenty-six mile marathons have become sissy stuff. Extreme endurance athletes are engaging in mind-numbing, backbreaking, tendon tearing, bone jarring, life-threatening events: ultra-marathons of up to several hundred miles, extreme cycling events that run days straight, multi-day "adventure racing" in the wilderness, and nine-mile swims.

There's a good chance that when the combined ravages of time and extreme endurance sports manage to double-team these over-the-top fitness fanatics, sixty may be the new ninety.

Suzuki and Me

A while back an article about the destructive effects of trawlers as they plunder the ocean bottom appeared in my column. The very scholarly article required extensive research, profound subject knowledge and deep personal conviction. Obviously I didn't write it.

The article appeared in my column *Lateral Thinking* because a computer, with its seemingly limitless capacity to extend the human capacity for error, cleverly deduced that the article by David Suzuki should appear as *Lateral Thinking* because his initials are the same as mine.

Readers plowed through the article waiting for the other shoe to drop ... for the funny side of man's pillage of the oceans to be revealed ... to find out what I thought was so hilarious about the destructive effects of man's greed.

The insertion of Suzuki's article in my column constituted a potentially crippling blow to my writing career just as it was starting to take off. My income from writing had already reached five figures ... counting the two following the decimal point. There's every indication that it was destined to skyrocket to the six figure level within a few decades, and that my readership could expand to dozens of people. I felt I had a brilliant future ahead in writing.

The blow to my writing career comes after an intense regime designed to strengthen my writing skills. I've trained hard by running on sentences, lifting passages, pumping irony, jumping to conclusions and stretching the truth. All for nothing!

On the surface, it might seem all right for readers to think I'm capable of writing serious articles which effectively make a point, but I'm worried about unfair expectations. Could my readers come to expect such things as relevant topics, correct sentence structure, multi-syllable words and clarity of thought? I hope not, but fear the worst. Yes, the error by the Enterprise may have ruined my reputation, but I'm hoping that this clarification minimizes the damage.

What if the shoe were on the other foot? How would David Suzuki feel if some of my tripe had been published in his column? Would his reputation as Canada's most charismatic and influential environmentalist and scientist be diminished if he were seen to promote a landfill site on a pristine trout lake in order to develop ecotourism?

Would he lose credibility for appearing to advocate the teaching of proper smoking techniques to our teenagers? Would he be pleased to find an article suggesting the development of unsafe streets to promote adventure tourism? All it takes is one careless click of the mouse and we'll know for sure.

Readers' Digest Bonanza

Be still, my pounding heart! I got a letter from an armoured car company. They may be delivering a check from Reader's Digest to my house. I may be the winner of the grand prize. Someone in Ontario may have won! It may be me!

A follow-up letter arrived... Big white envelop telling me to watch for the impending big blue envelop... Another contest ... or is it the same contest that started twenty years ago? It doesn't say ... the grand prize is coming soon ... entry forms ... special offers ... not everybody got these ... just special customers with elite status ... couple of car pictures, too... Just paste the plate numbers on the one I want and drop it in the envelop. I'm really close to the grand prize ... even bigger prize if I use the "YES" envelop to order the book on how to turn our living room into a beautiful one-stall garage. Whole forests were felled and postal employees suffered hernias to make all of this possible.

I was at home wondering if I should get a job so I could tell the boss to stuff it as soon as the megabucks arrive, when a friend called. After a bit of chatter, she said, "It's great to hear about all that new money!"

My first thought was, "I've won! The armoured car must have stopped at her house and asked for directions the Schwartz household in Ontario."

I guess I paused a bit too long and she continued, "You're still on the hospital board, aren't you? The government just announced some new money. The hospital has received more funding."

We chuckled over my first guess and then the idea hit me. Enter hospitals, personal care homes, and other public services in the Reader's Digest Sweepstakes. While administrators are meticulously drawing up budgets to address community needs, another team could be pasting stickers on contest forms. The more effective approach to fund vital services could be a toss-up. Perhaps, someday soon, an armoured ambulance will deliver sufficient funding to reopen needed care home beds.

Operating programs on government funding is a bit like building a lifestyle around anticipated Reader's Digest Sweepstakes winnings. Just like you're always on the verge of hitting the jackpot, governments announce special funding, don't release it, announce it again months later and so on. Finally, a pittance has been made to sound like enough to finance the Sponsorship Program's graft budget or keep the Governor General in pin money for a year.

Sonic Assault Forces Generation Ex Retreat

Trish and I went to a social a while back. You've gotta love socials. They're a great chance to visit and chat with old friends, have a few laughs and do some dancing. All this while supporting a worthwhile cause!

We arrived an hour before the band and were having a great time. The band arrived and started to play. Excellent music. Great musicians.

Played mostly boozegrass. We managed to visit, talk and dance a bit over the next hour as more people arrived.

Unfortunately for deafophobic conversaphiles, the band got louder by the minute! It seemed that they cranked the volume up whenever somebody tried to talk. It was soon impossible to communicate by any means other than sign language. I found myself saying, "Say it again, Sam," even though the person talking to me had both hands cupped around their mouth and was shouting into my ear.

For me, the music's too loud when I can't understand conversation from three feet away. I can compromise and bring that down to a foot or so but when my teeth start to rattle and I have to use sign language to get another beer, I'm ready to call The Police. We left in self-defence against someone taking the weed whacker to my cilia in another assault on my already compromised hearing.

The message we got was that if the music's too loud, you're too old. So we left, along with other members of Generation Ex and younger folks who wanted to live to hear another day.

What a waste! I had downed enough social lubricant to become a terrific dancer and a brilliant conversationalist with expertise on a wide range of topics. We wanted to stay and party but we enjoy music and conversation too much to jeopardize hearing them in the future.

The next day my ears were still ringing and I was still hoarse from futile yelling. We should have gone home sooner but would have saved ourselves a lot of frustration by staying home.

I can only guess at why so many bands play at ear-shattering volumes. They may be deaf from previous concerts and want to hear themselves. Perhaps they want to deafen more people so that deaf people feel less alone. They may take offence if you talk to someone while you should be honouring the Grateful Deaf. Or, perhaps those human pogo sticks posing as dancers are actually powered by bone-shaking music. In this case, the band was excellent, so it wasn't a matter of "If you can't play well, play loud." Whatever the reason, I've never heard of anyone leaving because the music wasn't loud enough.

Perhaps wearing protective muffs to events with blaring music would make a useful statement. Whoops. Bad idea. I'd look like the IBM nerd in a Mac ad. It would just illustrate the incredible coolness of loud music.

Garden Guard

The days are getting longer and we've been reminiscing about last year's garden and thinking about this year's. Our garden was a great success last summer, but not only for us. Like many fellow gardeners, we had trouble with various creatures sneaking into the garden and chowing down on the veggies. The raccoons enjoyed every cob of corn and the deer seemed bent on eating everything else. Elmer Fudd's nemesis, the Wascal Wabbit, also joined the party.

Some of the raiders came on two legs, though. A friend dropped by to visit on a beautiful summer day. We were away and the garden appeared to be unguarded. Tempted by the garden delectables, he took a step or two into the garden then recoiled at the sight of a slender green form slinking through the plants. He froze instantly when he saw that the end of the creature resembled the head of a cobra. Momentarily overcoming his fear, he took another step to get a better look.

"Pssst, pssst, pssst!" Hissing and spraying, the spitting cobra sprung into defence of its territory! The would-be garden raider managed to escape, enthusiasm and clothing dampened, and dignity shattered. His therapist says that he should recover from the posttraumatic stress and his emotional scars should heal after a few more visits.

He had unwittingly demonstrated the

effectiveness of our GDS (garden defence system). It's a pulse sprinkler that is activated by an infrared motion detector. When critters invade its territory, the sprinkler turns on, startles the intruder with sudden sound and zaps them with a spray of water. It's pretty effective. I know. It scared the bejeebers out of me every time I forgot about it and wandered into range. And I knew it was there.

The pulse sprinkler was the result of a decision that, since we were doing the work, we would like to sample at least some of the garden's bounty. The sprinkler followed a number of failed attempts to stop the raiders.

The Mark 1 GDS, brought into the battle a few years back, was a radio playing quietly in the garden. That worked for a few days until the CBC went on strike and started playing hours on end of soothing classical music. The deer were soon contentedly dining to music.

Next, since the deer came mainly at night, I coupled the radio to an electric light and a motion sensor aimed at the garden. The Mark 2 GDS was born. Deer entering the garden were scared off by the sudden display of light and sound. Worked like a charm! Unfortunately, the makeshift contraption was also activated by plants swaying in the wind. At every wind gust or animal visit, we were awakened by light and sound streaming into our bedroom window. So, we found out later, were the neighbours.

The chipmunks slip in under the radar,

however. They absolutely loved the strawberries, taking at least a bite out of every one in their version of Operation Dessert Storm

I've heard that old gardeners never die, they just spade away and throw in the trowel. Bad puns aside, those rats with antlers may have caused some gardeners to throw in the towel, but we're hanging in there and fighting back with weapons of pest reduction.

The Wizard of Poo

Our garden really sucked last year. While admiring the luxuriant growth in a friend's garden I was told that the secret of good plant performance is a happy social life. Plants appreciate a nice garden party with generous servings of tea.

Tea for plants is different. You put manure in a pail and add water. Then you allow the mixture to steep. The resulting brew is served to the plants by pouring it over them. They will then coyly sip the tea through their roots ... an apparent shyness comparable to that of winos who cleverly disguise their bottle in a paper bag while they sip.

Throwing a tea party in the garden seemed an easy way to provide a morale-booster for the food-production workers in our backyard food factory, so I set out to lay in the supplies.

At the store I was faced with a number of choices. Would my plants prefer cattle manure or sheep manure? "Bovine would be divine," I thought, and I set out to explore the remaining options. To my surprise, the steer and cow varieties were the only choices available. The frequently referenced bull stuff was conspicuously absent from the shelves. Nor could I find bags of the widely spread political variety.

Perhaps that's because it's of no more value to plants than to mainstream society.

I wanted only the best for our plants. On the

issue of quality, there was no information in Consumer Reports. However, I did know from milk ads that milk is better when it comes from contented cows. There was no information to be had on the relationship between a cow's contentment and quality of her dung. Given the human experience, one might expect negative correlation. At any rate, the manure bags did not make any claims about the emotional state of the cattle.

There was a choice of brand names, as well. I would have preferred President's Choice, had it been available. Unfortunately, the President had neglected to choose and I had to settle for Moo Poo or No-Name. I was swayed by the claim that Moo Poo contained 100% natural ingredients.

A large bag of Moo Poo cost only a couple of bucks. I was surprised that cattle work so cheaply.

As a socially conscious consumer, my concerns went beyond mere price and quality. There was also the issue of working conditions at the factory. Was calf labour being exploited? Were the cattle on the hundred-mile diet? Obviously, gender equality was a problem or there would have been bulls in the work force. Was this fair trade manure? All important questions for ethical consumers, but no answers were forthcoming from store personnel. I decided to hold my nose and go ahead anyway.

Right mooooove. The garden is fantastic this year!

Staying Found in the Woods

When one old woodsman was asked if he'd ever been lost, he replied, "No, but I once got a bit turned around for a week or so."

Getting lost in the bush can be a scary experience but once the lost soul is safely home, embarrassment and humiliation take over. It's hard to tell if the foundee's friends are glad he is safe or just delighted to have a fresh scapegoat for jokes and gibes. The newly-found will have a constant barrage of offers to guide him to the bathroom, to his back steps for the paper, or to work.

To avoid getting lost when traveling in the woods, some form of navigation system is necessary. Until recently, the most common navigation system available was the compass. Used in conjunction with a map, the compass could guide skilled woodsmen to their destination.

However, since many people don't know how to properly use a compass, the better models have a built-in mirror. The function of the mirror is to show the user who is lost and to make sure they look their best when the search party arrives.

Another less commonly used navigation method is based on the belief that moss always grows best on the north side of trees. People who use this system of navigation are generally referred to as lost.

Nothing has changed navigation for the

ordinary schmuck like the Global Positioning System. With a GPS, the average moron can flummox about the forest for hours and then, with the push of a button, head back directly to camp, the truck, or Grandma's house.

It's a good idea to have a back-up for the GPS just in case. You could use my recently developed TPS, or Trash Positioning System. (It started off as the Garbage Positioning System but the acronym was spoken for.) This low-tech navigational technique is foolproof because it requires no special equipment that you can forget at home. Although it doesn't work in pristine wilderness environments, it can guide you home if you're not too far from "civilization." It works best within an hour's drive of communities that charge tipping fees or require bag tags to dispose of waste.

The TPS works like this: Suppose you are flummoxing around in the bush and become disoriented. Sit down, calm down, look around. Look for trash. Get up and walk from garbage item to garbage item, noting the distance between items. If the litter is getting thicker, keep going in that direction. You're headed for town! You've been saved by idiots who think it's OK to dump their trash in the bush.

Honing your TPS skills will even enable you to determine what part of town you're approaching. For example, a thick carpet of cigarette butts and packages, pop cans and chip bags would signal proximity to a high school.

Who would have thought that the mentally lost who mark their trail with litter would be making the world more navigable for the rest of us? We owe them our gratitude. Ya think?

My Criminal Career

I didn't intend to. It just snuck up on me. I became a criminal on the first day of the new millennium.

Worried, I fled the country to find sanctuary and freedom in Castro's Cuba. I noticed a touch of irony after a couple of weeks and returned to Canada to turn myself in. Upon return, I found out that I was no longer a criminal! My temporary Firearms Possession Certificate had arrived. I had ordered it by mail order at the end of October during the big sale.

Great deal... 83% Off... a $60 "value" for just 10 loonies. Anyway, I'm a law-abiding citizen once more. I was a bit disappointed, as I was starting to enjoy the notoriety. However, the government's own estimates suggest that about a quarter million formerly law-abiding Canadians became instant criminals on January first. That should be enough notoriety to go around.

Critics denounce gun registration as a colossal waste of money. They say that Canada had excellent firearms legislation before, and that the new legislation is not going to reduce crime or make us any safer. True, but on the brighter side the new gun laws are going to make things better for hunters because it's going to be a whole lot harder for crooks to go hunting. Hunters will no longer have to share the woods with criminals. It's comforting to know that criminals will be on the streets where they belong.

The flip side isn't so bright. Criminals will be safer. The hundreds of millions (soon to be billions) spent on gun registration will mean less police to fight crime and many will be stuck in the office pushing paper around to register all those guns and prosecute all the instant criminals. But when Hell finally freezes, the criminals will turn in their illegal weapons and we'll all be safer. I can hardly wait!

A Penny Saved is a Penny Spurned

I was self-employed for a while last year. It worked out well. I cleared a cool $7,200 per hour … tax-free! That's nearly $29 million per year! Take home! Didn't even have to work overtime! Not bad for a retired guy!

Since I'm not a sports hero, you might think I own a Quebec advertising agency with Liberal connections, and I've been cashing in on the sponsorshit program. Actually, I only made two bucks. My brief period of "self-employment" lasted about a second ... the time required to pick a toonie off the sidewalk. Two bucks in one second is $7,200 an hour. Do the math. Too bad it didn't last longer. I always thought toonies should have been called doubloonies to capture the relationship to the loonie and mix in a hint of the dubloon of lost Spanish treasure legends. Toonie is so lame. But I digress.

Taking a second of your busy day to scoop up a stray loony pays $3,600 per hour, and quarters net $900. Even pennies don't pay that badly. If you're slow at it, you should still be able to snag one off the ground and pocket it in a couple of seconds: $18 an hour ... tax free. But nobody stoops to that.

The old adage, "a penny saved is a penny earned," doesn't have much credibility any more. Pennies buy so little that most people don't even bother to spend them, much less pick them up. If you actually stood in a checkout line and counted out pennies to pay for even a small purchase, someone would probably go into change rage.

If there are any pennies in your pocket right now, you probably received them as change today. When you get home with them, you'll squirrel them away in a jar in your dresser or under the bed. You'll hoard them for years, perhaps hoping to someday forge them into new plumbing pipes or copper jewelry. Your pockets will be penniless when you start your next day. A penny saved is a penny spurned.

No wonder! A whole pound of pennies might buy a cup of designer coffee. Money isn't supposed to outweigh what you can buy with it, so pennies aren't a convenient medium of exchange. If you've got a load of pennies in your pocket, it might help you to walk in a cross-wind, but that's about it.

All those useless pennies cost a bundle to make. Why isn't Stephen Harping about a Common Cents Revolution to axe the penny? Where's Mike Harris when we need him? Lose the penny and find taxpayer's dollars!

Mondegreen Madness

Recently, I was the master of ceremonies at a retirement celebration at which there were a number of songs, anecdotes and tributes by various contributors. Some of the participants were identified only in the final moments before the formalities started. As a result, my agenda, hastily completed, was cobbled together on a scrap of paper. That's my excuse and I'm sticking with it!

Early in the program, I was introducing a singing group, the Kubasonics, and the chief organizer and stage director was prompting, "No, Nancy is next."

"Dancing is next," I announced. "Nancy is next!" came the prompt. "Yes, bring on the dancing!" I replied.

After several more exchanges, I finally invited Dancing Nancy to the stage to do her presentation.

Such mondegreen-related events add variety to my life. Strictly speaking, the word "mondegreen" refers to the mis-hearing of a popular phrase or song lyric. However, I prefer to extend the definition to include everything I mishear and that's lots, due to high frequency hearing loss that makes it difficult to hear consonants. I hear the vowels and guess at the gaps.

The term mondegreen was coined by writer Sylvia Wright. As a child she had listened to the

Scottish ballad "The Bonny Earl of Murray" and heard one verse this way: "Ye Highlands and Ye Lowlands, Oh where hae you been? They hae slay the Earl of Murray, And Lady Mondegreen." What they had actually done was "slay the Earl of Murray and lay him on the green." Her tragic heroine ceased to exist when Wright discovered the truth. As a result, she coined the new word.

Most mondegreens come from song lyrics. Imagine driving along with your legs pinched together, desperately needing relief and being teased by the radio blaring, "There's a bathroom on the right," a common mishearing of "There's a bad moon on the rise" from the song "Bad Moon Rising" by Credence Clearwater Revival. That's a first class mondegreen!

More examples include Bob Dylan's lyrics, "Dead ants are my friends, they're blowin' in the wind," Crystal Gayle's "Doughnuts Make Your Brown Eyes Blue," Jimmy Buffet's "Let's get Drunk at School" and the popular hymn "Gladly the Cross-Eyed Bear."

You can check your dictionary for "mondegreen," but if you don't find it, it might only prove that it's time for a new dictionary.

The New Apathetic Party

If you're anything like me, and I know I am, you're agonizing over who to vote for in the coming election. You're suffering through those endless, painful debates, listening to Stephen Harping about the Liberal culture of entitlement. The die-hard party faithful, be they Convertibles (think Belinda), Fiberals, Blockheads, or New Democrats, aren't faced with the dilemma. They know well in advance how they will vote. Lucky them. Their party could run a thieving, drunken, pedophilic serial axe-murderer and the true party faithful line up to vote for them. Sometimes when entire ridings are dominated by such people we have what are called safe seats.

There's another group who aren't faced with a dilemma ... those who won't bother to vote. An estimated 42% of eligible voters in the coming election won't show up. Amazing! 70% of Iraqis dodged suicide bombers and bullets in order to vote. Over 40% of Canadians will be deterred by hangnails, icy sidewalks or bad hair days.

The apathetic need a party that represents their disinterests ... a party consisting of the totally uninvolved. It would be called the New Apathetic Party. NAP memberships would be automatically given to those who didn't vote in the last election.

Choosing candidates for NAP will be a bit of a challenge, as will the selection of a leader. The

Lazy-Boy chairs at the NAP leadership convention, however, will be the envy of the other parties.

Naturally, NAP would not make, never mind break, any election promises. This would be refreshing and appeal to many potential non-voters. There would be no inane gimmicks like the promise to completely ban handguns and make it a crime to have one. For almost everyone, it's already a crime to possess a handgun. NAP, of course, would promise nothing. Under NAP, all crime would simply continue to be illegal.

Uncast ballots would be considered a vote for the NAP candidate. If the percentage of people not casting their ballot exceeded that voting for any of the other candidates, the NAPSTER would be declared elected.

You may be skeptical about this idea but it's as workable as many of the promises we're hearing from the other parties. They are lambasting us with weapons of mass deception, bombarding us with new versions of the loaves and fishes trick. Promises of tax cuts accompany promises of gazillions in new spending on everything imaginable, all adding up to massive budget surpluses.

Something doesn't add up. If you fool people to get their money, it's crime. If you fool them to get their vote, it's just good politics. It's enough to drive you to NAP. But get out there and vote anyway!

Ha-ha

"I smell something funny."

"Ha-ha funny, or oh-oh funny?"

"Don't know yet. I'm stopping to look." Then seconds later, came, "Make that oh-oh funny. My truck's on fire!"

That was the gist of the radio conversation between two drivers when a logging truck caught fire on the English River Road. The fire quickly spread to the nearby forest. The forest fire was water bombed and extinguished within minutes, providing a great air show for the drivers. The truck and its load of logs burned completely, leaving only charred remains of frame and engine. Definitely not "ha-ha funny."

There's usually nothing funny when something's "oh-oh funny." However, it's funny how we use the same word in two such different ways.

Imagine a car travelling on a curving, shoulderless section of Railway Street, with mailboxes and hydro poles very close to the travelled portion. The driver's happily chatting on a cell phone and munching on Tim Bits. Multitasking at its finest and most dangerous!

"I just heard a funny thump," the driver remarks. "Ha-ha funny, or oh-oh funny?" comes the reply.

Looking in the mirror, the driver replies, "Oh-oh funny. I just bumper-stuffed a pedestrian into a roadside mailbox. If he's headed for the hereafter, I sure hope it's by expedited post."

It's funny how the City of Kenora has, for many years, overlooked the very dangerous conditions for non-motorized traffic on Railway Street. Sooner or later, it could be oh-oh funny. Funnier still, how much public pressure is required to bring about safety improvements so obviously necessary and so long overdue. Now that improvements seem about to happen, let's hope it's not "Oh-oh, too little," or "Oh-oh, too late."

Another funny thing: Driving while yakking on cell phones has proved more deadly than drunken driving, but our government still hasn't banned the practice. That example of oh-oh funny has already cost many lives.

It's a funny thing when funny isn't funny. Oh-oh, I may have wet myself laughing.

Eats Shoots and Leaves

One fall I got a new nickname. By sheer good luck (for me, not the moose), I bagged a bull moose an hour after the hunting season opened. The fun was over and the work began. It took my hunting partners and I the rest of the day to skin, quarter, wrap, and lug the quarters to our hunting camp. We hung it to cool overnight, festooned with bells, pots and pans to wake us if bears decided to have a midnight snack. It was hot by noon the next day, and I had to take the meat to a butcher shop. I wolfed down a great lunch, bid my hunting buddies good luck and headed for town. Because I'd stuck my partners with the job of dismantling the hunt camp and packing up, I was promptly dubbed "Panda."

The new moniker was a takeoff on a joke in which a panda walks into a restaurant, eats a good meal, fires a few gunshots into the ceiling and walks out without paying. Later, when the cops apprehended him, the panda explained that this was expected behaviour. In the animal behaviour book, under panda, was the caption, "Eats, shoots, and leaves." Pandas, of course, really do eat shoots and leaves. The joke is used to illustrate how a comma can dramatically change the meaning of a sentence.

Eats, Shoots, and Leaves is also the title of very humorous book on proper punctuation to which I should pay more attention. But I digress. Nicknames are usually short, clever, cute or derogatory substitute names for a person's real name. A couple dandies that spring to mind are "Logfather" (oldest guy on his logging crew) and "Johnny Nocash" (perpetually broke). Another nickname, "Crash," probably earned but well short of flattering or confidence-inspiring for that pilot's passengers.

There's often a funny story behind a person's nickname. Consider the canoe tripper who always had one more little task to do before getting back in the canoe. It didn't matter when or where the group stopped, for how long or why. The poor gal was just never ready to leave. Careful observation revealed that whenever the decision came get into the canoes and go, she had to go. She soon became known as Never-ready. That quickly expanded to Never-ready the Pissageyser Bunny, who just keeps on ... would you believe talking and talking?

Pissed Off with Profanity

Every once in a while, I manage to piss somebody off. Well, OK, so it's more than once in a while, but it's definitely not everybody. Well, OK, maybe it's everybody. But for sure it's not everybody all of the time. As a great pundit once got misquoted, "You can piss off some of the people some of the time and all of the people some of the time, but you can't piss off all of the people all of the time." Even Osama Bin Laden didn't manage that.

I must apologize to my genteel readers for using an expression that may be considered vulgar, but isn't it a great expression? Sometimes "annoy" or "peeve" just don't cut it.

It does puzzle me that "piss" should be considered profane. I actually had to tell my spell-checker to learn a word that is more suitable than any of its alternatives. Say it right and the sound of the word mimics that of the action itself. For contrast, take aim into the bowl and try to create the sound of "urinate" or "pass water."

I normally try to avoid profanity, dismissing it as the sound of a weak mind trying to express itself, but I am prone to failure for obvious reasons. The difference between intention and reality means that I sometimes resort to off-colour expressions in the search for descriptive terminology.

Perhaps the boundaries of profanity need adjusting. If there's room in the dictionary for "hottie," just added to the North American lexicon, to refer to a physically attractive person, then surely we can make room for the p-word to be used in polite company.

But I digress. To get to the point, assuming there's one, sometimes I vex someone (see what I mean?) so badly that they quit talking to me. I hope those folks are so alienated (can't overuse the more effective expression) that they don't read my column. I don't want them to find out how much my life improves when we aren't on speaking terms. They could start talking to me again just to make me miserable. I'm really taking a chance by writing this.

Isn't it wonderful when some idiot (a better term exists but I'll let propriety prevail on this one) sticks their nose in the air and punishes you with the gift of their silence! The reason might be a difference of opinion. They think that they, and everyone else on the planet, are entitled to their opinion. Often they are bores whose presence deprives you of solitude but fails to provide company. When they walk out of a room it feels like someone really interesting has just stepped in. You know the type. They know everything. Except that they are a bore!

Lard of the Rinks

An estimated half a million men play recreational hockey in Canada. The risk of heart attack related to this is estimated at 10 deaths per winter.

People buy lottery tickets with much worse odds of collecting but the rewards of fun, camaraderie and fitness far outweigh the risks.

I had a scary experience recently while playing hockey.

I had worked up a good sweat, my breath was coming in rasping gasps and my heart was pounding.

Suddenly, everything went black.

"Oh-oh, this can't be good," I thought. I anticipated hovering over my own body, watching the guys do CPR and dial 911 on their cell phones. Others would rush off to get the defibrillator to give me a jump-start.

One of them with advanced first aid training would shout, "Stand back, everybody back!"

The risk of heart attack for liniment league players had been refreshed in my mind by yet another fear-inspiring news article. I was expecting the worst and waiting for a light beckoning at the end of a long tunnel.

Strangely, there was no pain.

After a few seconds things started returning to normal. The rink slowly regained its brightness as the mercury vapour lights warmed up again after a brief power outage. Meanwhile, the guys compared out-of-body experiences. Finally, play resumed.

Most of the goal-den boys I play with are in their fifth, sixth, and even seventh decade of hockey. In this decadent bunch, dry-land training has been replaced by dry-out training and everybody gives ten percent. A good game means there have been no sudden deaths in regulation time and everyone gets to the coffee shop on two legs and can still rub both eyes with both hands.

When a match ends in a tie, it's left that way for fear that new meaning will be given to the term sudden death overtime. As in the NHL, the winner will be decided by a shoot-out. However, for us, it will be a verbal shoot-out at the coffee shop.

As revered athletes, we have a lot of supporters. They are not, however, cheering wildly from the stands or hanging out at the door of the rink waiting for autographs. Our supporters are loyally waiting in stinky equipment bags to brace knees, ankles and other ailing joints.

Old-timers' hockey continues to bloom even as the geriatric jocks who play it are going to seed. With such popularity there should be a movie about the old boys of winter. It could build on the success of *Grumpy Old Men* and *Slap Shot* and focus on the quest for the Brown Bottle, the fun-league answer to the Grey Cup.

The movie name? *Flab Shot*, *Oldblood* and *Net Worst* came to mind. Those possibilities were quickly dismissed when I took a look around the dressing room. The movie would have to be called Lard of the Rinks.

Lard of the Rinks- The Sequel

Without truth there can be no humour. However, the truth can be stretched, distorted and diluted at the whim of the wannabe humourist. Nobody expects the real straight goods in a humour column. At least I hope not.

The truth, the whole truth, and nothing but the truth usually just won't cut it. The truth usually needs embellishments and some twisting to make a funny story.

Anyway, truth was at a bare minimum in my recent column *Lard of the Rinks*. I took a lot of flak about that from my fellow geriatric jocks, so I should clarify a few things.

The lights did actually go off while I was playing hockey with the Sunday morning hockey group. There were anxious moments as ten guys suddenly lost sight of where they were while were careening around the ice at top speed, Fortunately everyone got stopped without injury, but it was scary. The potential for serious injuries was very real.

Top speed on skates, even for geriatric jocks, is quite fast, though not fast enough that slow motion replays would be of great value. However, admissions that some of the weekend warriors still have wheels are of little value in a humour piece. Better to describe play as proceeding at a glacial pace.

Until the lights were bright enough for us to resume play there was some ease-the-tension joking. The levity included variations of the theme, "When everything went black I thought, oh-oh, this can't be good."

The article's claim that the old boys of winter give 10 percent pokes fun at the absurd, but frequent reference to the pros put out 110 percent. The real truth is that at old-timers hockey, the guys are putting out their full 100 percent, just like the pros. It's just a question of 100 percent of what.

My own terror when everything went black was pure fabrication. I was sitting safely on the bench at the time. You can't poke fun at that. The comment about my heart pounding wildly as my breath came in rasping gasps, however, was only slightly exaggerated as I had just finished my shift. The incident happened just after Christmas, so I had been skating with a turkey around my midriff. It was probably the fastest he's ever gone unless you count the truck ride to the packing plant

It was the suggestion that a movie about the old boys of winter be called *Lard of the Rinks* that caused stuff to hit the fan. The truth is that most of the guys are in pretty good shape despite having traded the rippling six-packs of their youth for Molson muscle. The washboard stomachs have been replaced by washtub stomachs. But what's funny about older guys being in shape? Other than the fact that pear is a shape.

A Most Delightful Misery

Every once in a while, I just have to get away from it all. I grow weary of the constant comfort and convenience of modern life and crave relief from soft beds, central heating and cooling, elevators, hot showers, mud-free, flat and level sidewalks and delicious food served at a real table while I'm seated on a real chair.

I can escape the cloying comfort of modern existence by going camping. Camping provides a truly fine and pleasant misery while I reconnect with the natural world and experience the hardships of my forbearers.

Camping comes in varying levels of deprivation and discomfort to suit all tastes. At the entry level is the recreational vehicle (RV) or travel trailer in which all the comforts and conveniences of home accompany the "campers" as they are powered along from campground to campground by releasing the energy of stored sunshine. The level of sacrifice is minuscule in these contrivances and has no legitimate claim to association with true camping misery. In my view, anything that requires a gas generator isn't camping.

These motorized comfy-campers may not have to endure the rigours of camping but they do manage to ruin the experience of camping purists and nature lovers with the semi-muffled chugs of their gas generators drowning out the sounds of nature and with the flickering light of their large screen TVs ruining the view of the night sky. It causes me to wonder if they are watching nature shows late into the night to complete their reconnection with nature at the national park.

To experience misery worthy of the title, Trish and I camp in a tent. At the beginner level of tenting discomfort, we would travel to a campground by car. Unfortunately, the vehicle begs for the inclusion of sufficient creature comforts to prevent a credible degree of misery. For example, including a camp stove would cheat us out the experience of cooking over an open fire, pungent smoke wafting into ours eyes and noses causing stinging tear-filled eyes and violent fits of coughing.

Similarly, taking along an airbed would cause us to miss the therapeutic pain of Mother Earth, unhampered by an adequate mattress, jabbing at us viciously with roots and rocks as we're being kept awake all night by the sounds of our surroundings. These night noises, undiminished by rigid walls and windows, include, but are certainly not limited to, the inane ravings of drunken revelry in the neighbouring campsites or the ominous snuffling of bears. To bears, humans in sleeping bags are Mother Nature's own soft tacos.

Rising at dawn, usually because I can't stand lying awake any longer, I emerge from the tent to savour the glory of the breaking day. This is popularly known as getting up to take a leak and is usually accompanied by a furious onslaught of biting insects waiting in ambush to desanguinate me.

Of course, whatever the level of tenting discomfort, there's also the possibility of having to emerge from the tent in a driving rainstorm to answer nature's call. From the comfort perspective, the deluge usually keeps the mosquitos at bay.

Having opted for a tent, it's possible to raise the misery index by backpacking or paddling into the backcountry where no Winnebago or Airstream dares to tread. Of these, paddling is the lesser intrusion on comfort and sanity because adventurers only have to carry the mountain of gear on the back-breaking portages between lakes or around rapids. The rest of the time it just floats blissfully along in the canoe or kayak as we flail ourselves to exhaustion on the paddles.

Opting instead for a multi-day backpacking trip packs a double whammy on the misery index. Because I have to fit everything in a pack on my back, the mattress gets thinner, the tent more cramped and the food less palatable. The seemingly interminable daily trudge is broken only by the need to set up camp again and eat some disgusting dried food. Despite my best efforts to restrict the volume and weight of my pack, it will grind me down until the only sign of my passage is that of my butt dragging along the trail.

Of course. the tribulation index can be enhanced by opting for wilderness camping by canoe or backpack. Fortunately, this wards off any phone zombies who might want to tag along, enabled by cell phone service and the possibility of a timely helicopter rescue.

At the pinnacle of discomfort and misery is winter camping. Tents may be forsaken in favour of snow huts called quinzhees. Making and sleeping in one of these winter hovels definitely takes misery to a level which is beyond the scope of this article. One of the special delights of winter camping is a blazing fire around which campers attempt to warm themselves. Around this inferno, one can have the unique discomfort of being too hot and too cold simultaneously. Only one side at a time can face the fire and will be heated nearly to ignition temperature while the other side freezes.

There's one comforting aspect of winter camping, though. The mosquito abatement program is flawless.

Discount Dilemma

The only thing consistent about me is my inconsistency. I've always refused to claim the senior's discount available at many stores and restaurants. As I'm normally a bargain hunter, the paradoxical behaviour can only be a result of my reluctance to admit the onset of geezerhood. That's another paradox when you consider that I eagerly broke into old-timers' hockey as an under-aged player about forty years ago.

I was in a check-out line the other day and couldn't help overhearing the octogenarian just ahead of me complaining that he had bought something earlier in the day and hadn't received his seniors' discount. He was informed that he had to tell the cashier that he was a senior and then he would receive the discount. They would make the refund this time but in the future he must remember to point out that he is a senior. The instruction was immediately repeated in case the old geezer had already forgotten.

Of course he must tell them. They aren't detectives. How else would they know that a stooped and wrinkled, white-haired gentleman is a senior?

He might be a twenty-something who has lived too much in the fast lane. Worse yet, he could be a fraud artist disguised as an old man just to get a ten percent discount on his purchase of Geritol and Polygrip.

My turn arrived and the cashier rang up my

purchase. I produced the cash along with a mischievous inquiry about how old a person had to be to get a seniors' discount.

"Fifty-five, sir," she said.

"How old would a person have to look in order to receive it automatically," I asked, trying to conceal my amusement.

"Sixty-five, sir," she replied, handing me my change.

I nodded my head up and down as the change snapped in and out of focus through my every-step's-an-adventure quadrafocals. Once I had located the correct head position, a quick count revealed that I had received my first ever senior's discount. But I still didn't ask for it.

Waking up to Sleep's Benefits

Surveys indicate that two-thirds of Canadian workers admit to sleepiness interfering with their work. Actually, those are the American figures, but a Canadian expert, caught napping on the issue, confirmed that Canadian figures would be similar. The cost of workplace drowsiness to Canadian employers could be in the order of two billion dollars in lost productivity and accidents.

Waking up to the problem, one Canadian company has created "alertness recovery rooms," that have couches, reclining chairs and alarm clocks. Employees on twelve-hour night shifts, who need to, are permitted to doze off for fifteen minutes with the company's blessing. "Alertness recovery" has the potential to become the buzzword of the millennium.

Other companies are developing similar schemes that permit workers to get fired-up for napping, instead of just fired. However, there's still a stigma attached to sleeping on the job, and companies that provide a place for employees to nap are keeping it under the covers, disguised by names like "alertness recovery room." A couple of personal suggestions are "drowsiness reversal modules" and "proactive perceptiveness enhancement chamber." Unfortunately, the term "rest room" has already been claimed by another serious threat to modern productive efficiency. Government ministries could be consulted to provide a full range of suitably obfuscating terminology.

Workplace naps are actually a recycled old idea from a kinder and fatter era that contrasts with the present leaner and meaner times and its sacred mantra of competition. Back in the fifties, my grandfather's small-town general store had a back room with a couch and Grandpa freely and openly engaged in "alertness recovery therapy," but most thought he was just nodding off.

Day care workers and kindergarten teachers have been on to the idea of naps to increase productivity for years. It really is high time that industry caught up.

In the modern workplace regular naps will have to be replaced by power naps. Power naps fit the concept of a competitive environment very nicely. Snoozing does not. Picture a highly competitive executive at the peak of his career flexing powerful eyelids, resolving to out-rest the competition and, perhaps, snore them into submission. Imagine training seminars with teams of employees attending lectures by renowned nap gurus and psyching themselves up to rest faster and more effectively than the opposition. This is competitive relaxation at its best! It could become an Olympic event!

Staying in Shape

I'll do anything for a great body except diet and exercise. –Steve Martin

It's October 5th. The wind is howling. It's snowing. Hard. Despite the weather, I'm out for a run, as limbered up as I get, and just settling into a steady pace. In front of me the snow is starting to accumulate on the ground. The wind is whipping up whitecaps on the lake. The first snowfall of the season. Bummer!

I'm bootin' it right along at a pretty good pace, for me. Starting to puff a bit. I play on a drinking team with a hockey problem. Season starts in two weeks. Gotta get in shape!

Running on my left is a young chick. Fiftyish, I think. She's got a really weird gait ... runs flat-footed in a sort of bounding motion. Her arms are flailing in a goofy back and forth motion. What's more, she's keeping right up with me. I pick up the pace.

Further to my left is a young woman wearing a tank top. In this weather! She's running backwards and keeping up with me. She's a looker, too!

She's looking at a magazine, flipping through the pages. There are articles with titles like "Seven Minutes to Buns of Steel," "Lose 100 Pounds in Two Weeks or Die Trying" and "1,199 Exciting New Moves to Try in Bed Tonight." It's loaded with pictures of steel buns, rippling six-packs, tans to die for (a real possibility) and eye-catching silicone containers.

There's half a dozen of us running abreast. I spot someone cycling straight toward us from the side, oblivious to where he's headed. He's pedaling toward us like a madman possessed by road rage. Nothing happens.

I spot a creaky looking old geezer reflected in a window. Looks like a po0ster-boy for 'The Old and the Listless.' I'm flabbygasted. He's keeping up! I must be losing it! Macho instincts force me to pick up the pace. So does he! Wait a minute ... it's my reflection in the window.

The Lakeside Inn looms up in front of me through the window of the Michael Smith Fitness Centre. I'm on a treadmill. Its dashboard belongs in a jet fighter. Digital readouts blaze out information about speed, pulse, zone and fat burn. Just one more hour at this pace, and I'll have burned of an extra helping of Thanksgiving dinner. In advance! Heck with it. I punch the stop button. That extra helping will have to go to waist.

The Man in the Cardboard Dress

Trish and I dropped in at a friend's rural home for a visit a while ago. I knocked at the door and got no response. His vehicle was at home so we knew he wasn't far away.

We honked the horn and waited. Finally, he appeared from behind a building wearing nothing but a big grin, rubber boots and the cardboard shipping carton from a clothes dryer. He managed a briefless, brief conversation in which he assured us that he had not just returned from a poker game. He had been enjoying the backyard sauna, his personal, clothing optional retreat and hadn't taken any clothing along. He apologized for keeping us waiting but it had taken time to find something to make himself presentable. Presentable perhaps, but definitely an unconventional fashion statement.

It can be embarrassing to arrive at some event and find that you are making an unconventional fashion statement. I know this from personal experience. I have a knack for showing up in a suit when everyone else is in t-shirts and jeans. If the rest of the crowd is dressed to the nines, expect me to arrive in my painting clothes.

Even going out to get a bit of exercise can land you in sartorial shame. It seems that every sport or activity is getting its own specialized clothing. Going for a bike ride demands cycling-specific spandex. Cross-country skiing (one hopes this is restricted to narrow countries) has its own specialized skin-tight spandex. Show up for a loppet in wool knickers or at a bike race in baggy sweatpants and you'll look dorkier than the IBM guy in a Mac ad.

Hats off to nudists, though. I bet they make the right fashion statement every time. There's no doubt about what to wear to a nudist event.

Whether it's cycling, volleyball, fine dining or just hanging out at the beach, your one-button suit will be the perfect ensemble. Finding a place to put your keys might be your biggest problem. If that kind of fashion simplicity appeals to you, you'll have to go south to live out your dreams.

Bare butts may be cool, but all Canadian destinations are clothed for the winter.

A nude vacation would also simplify air travel. You could cut down on luggage and still have the perfect ensemble for all occasions.

No naturist retreat for me, though. I'll stick with the prude beach. Too many wrinkles in the birthday suit.

And the Darwin Award Almost Went to ... Nuisance Humans

If you're reading this (a strong possibility under the circumstances), you aren't, at least not yet, a candidate for a Darwin Award. Your choice of reading material, however, clearly demonstrates the required intelligence.

In the spirit of Charles Darwin, the Darwin Awards are bestowed posthumously on individuals who eliminate themselves from the gene pool in some spectacular misapplication of judgment. In this way, provided they have no offspring yet, they improve the chances for the long-term survival of our species.

Past recipients include a terrorist who mailed a letter bomb with insufficient postage. He blew himself up upon opening the returned package. The fisherman who threw a lit stick of dynamite that his faithful golden retriever fetched and returned to him was also a winner. You can easily see that the standards are very high and that great personal sacrifice is necessary to qualify for the prestigious award.

A couple of years back, a tourist to the area made a gallant attempt to qualify for a Darwin Award. The dummy had Smarties and was feeding them to a roadside bear while his friends videotaped the action.

Unfortunately, the bear's appetite outlasted the Smarties and it mauled the dummy before being scared away by people who put their own lives at risk to prevent a true Darwinian performance. Police had no alternative but to shoot the bear and send its brain to be tested for rabies. They may have been testing the wrong brain for the wrong disorder.

If a bear doesn't high-tail it long before you get really close, it might be one of those MNR decoy bears trying to trick you into breaking the game laws. More likely, it's a bear that has lost its natural fear of humans, viewing them as the ninety-eight pound weaklings of the forest. The bear in this incident must have had some good reason why it didn't want to leave when the tourist approached ... probably munchies ... a great patch of grass, road salt or a deer carcass.

I bet the last few seconds of that video tape are a real hoot, not that it's funny when someone gets mauled by a bear. Neither is it funny when a beautiful animal has to be destroyed because of someone's foolishness.

A lot of effort is made to keep humans safe from bears, to the extent of trapping nuisance bears in the city and releasing them in the wild. Maybe that's backwards! How about trapping nuisance humans in the wild and releasing them in their natural urban environment where they can live without endangering wildlife and their fellow humans?

Maybe the Ministry of Natural Resources decoy bear can be used to identify the nuisance humans.

Shucks! Not More Inukshuks

Inukshuks have been popping up around Sunset Country like new friends around a lottery winner. They gaze down at us from the hilltops, stare at us from the roadside and even peer up at us from the bottom of ditches. We've all seen these out-of-place rock piles and wondered what their builders were thinking.

The traditional purpose of inukshuks may be a clue to the riddle. Inukshuk is an Inuit word meaning manlike in appearance and refers to rock cairns constructed to resemble people. One of the traditional functions of the inukshuks was, and still is, to serve as navigation aids in a vast and treeless land with few natural landmarks. Even klutzy Southerners can sometimes use them effectively. When canoeing in the North, whenever we came to an expanse of water that we needed to cross, we would scan the horizon for inukshuks. If we could spot an inukshuk on the other shore, we could paddle toward it with assurance that it was marking the entrance to a channel.

Could the builders of the local roadside sentinels be putting them there to guide navigationally-challenged drivers? Motorists who can't follow roads can follow the friendly hillside guides with confidence that they are on the highway and not an airport runway or a parking lot. Roadside inukshuks provide reassurance that the hard grey surface with the yellow and white lines really is the road!

Another traditional function of inukshuks was to assist in hunting. From a distance, several rocks piled one on top of the other on the crest of a treeless ridge look amazingly like a person standing there. Apparently caribou think so, too. They could be herded between two rows of inukshuks and funneled toward hunters waiting in ambush.

Could the purpose of those roadside monuments be to herd vehicles along the road, preventing them from piling into the rock-cuts, ditches or the bush by threatening them from the roadside? Are drivers who might witlessly veer off the road being herded, caribou-like, along the road by the rock structures looming above them on the roadside? Or could the inukshuks be part of a police conspiracy to herd unsuspecting speeders into a waiting radar trap ambush?

Are they symbols of the budding artistic talent and intelligence of local residents? Look tourists, we can make rock piles! Stop and explore our developing culture!

The mystery unfolds. Having experienced inukshuks in their natural Arctic habitat, I find that I am annoyed by their constant intrusion. Paradoxically, I plan to construct a beautiful, big inukshuk at the end of our driveway. It will guide me home after those late nights and greet me when even the dog won't.

Round and Roundabout We Go

City council is giving us the roundabout again. This time it's a real one: a roundabout is being planned for our busiest intersections.

Opponents of Kenora's roundabout warn of impending doom. According to them, the end of civilization won't be caused by Britney's next wardrobe omission or global warming. It will be the roundabout that brings civilization to its knees. That circle of doom will be a black hole into which cars, trucks, cyclists and pedestrians disappear, never to re-emerge.

To allay fears, special features could be added to the design. The centre island could have a crash-activated body bag dispenser and emergency ration kits for stranded truckers. A post-traumatic stress counsellor could be stationed at each exit in case anyone gets out alive.

In my opinion, the roundabout is great for that location. With good design, it will move traffic safely and efficiently. However, this one looks like a Rube Goldberg car-crusher. Fortunately, if the engineers messed up, it can be rebuilt at our expense.

With half the city singing the blues about it, the roundabout saga rates its own song. Try the following lyrics to the tune of "Oh dear what can the matter be."

Oh Dear, what is the fuss about?
The whole City Council is lost in the roundabout
They'll circle the issue 'til they burn all their gas out
And everyone said they'd be there

The first to get there was our mayor Compton
To lead the circle who else could you count on
He'll go round and round 'til he burns all the gas out
And everyone knows he's there

Oh Dear, what is the fuss about?
Three police forces are lost in the roundabout
They'll go round and round 'til they burn their gas out
And everyone knows they are there

The next to arrive were two high school systems
They circle both ways to offer more options
Duplicating each other 'til they burn all our cash up
And nobody knows why they're there

The next on the scene was a busload of tourists
They'd come 'cross the country to check out the Big Spruce
They'll go round and round 'til they burn all the gas out
And everyone knows they are there

The next to get there were folks for the market
Who would buy some veggies if they just could park it
They'll go round and round 'til the lettuce is wilted
And everyone knows they are there

The roundabout is part of the "Big Spruce" that is now taking root downtown. The Big Spruce is the face-lift that's going to beautify Kenora, enrich our lives and be our economic salvation. There's been lots of controversy over the Big Spruce. We're spending big bucks on cosmetics when the economy is in the sewer.

Splurging to make our city more attractive to tourists and businesses or professionals who might locate here, has opposition.

Critics of the Big Spruce maintain that we're in dire economic straits. We should tighten our belts, pinch our pennies and ride things out until prosperity magically returns. These may be the same people who, if out of work, would quit buying soap, combs and razor blades until they finally get a job that pays well.

The austerity approach could work. Do nothing. Let Kenora wither away and become a ghost town. Since ghost towns are incredible tourist magnets, legions of visitors would put us back on the gravy train. But then we'd no longer be a ghost town! Vicious circle ... sort of like a roundabout.

The Roundabout Revolution

The roundabout is just about up and circling. One more exit to open and we'll be the proud owners of Northwestern Ontario's first roundabout. Kenora is making history again.

Now that the rubber has hit the road, the roundabout is working just fine. Human nature is funny. Perhaps I'm convinced it's working because I always said it would. Those who said all along that the sky would fall still swear adamantly that it isn't working. I manage to see traffic moving smoothly, even during Kenora's rush minute. The nay sayers see the same traffic backed up for miles. Nobody likes to be wrong and many of us will argue that red is green in order to appear right.

The final test will be when the rubber no longer hits the road due to layers of ice and piles of snow. Big rigs winding their way through in the worst winter conditions will be the true test. Truckers are skeptical but there is hope that their worst fears may be unjustified, given the invention of snow-moving equipment.

When the roundabout first opened I pedaled over there to try it out. I circled left 450 degrees to turn right onto Veteran's Drive, then returned to do a 540 degree turn, straight through onto Bernier. Then I stopped to watch.

Drivers were also acting loopy. Most made a round or two before they decided to exit, usually sporting an ear-to-ear grin. Looked like they were training for Nascar. Go fast, turn left. They were either just horsing around or happy to emerge alive from the terrifying circle of doom. In any case, there were no missing persons reports.

On the green side, it takes 40% less fuel to go through a roundabout than a regular intersection. Take that, critics! The fuel saving alone should pay the thing off within centuries, not to mention the other environmental benefits.

Safety benefits of roundabouts are being negated by drivers operating mobile phone booths with a food counter and a license to kill as they chat away and sip their coffee on the fly.

Fortunately, roundabout rage has occurred only in letters to the editor. What happened to making your words soft and sweet in case you have to eat them?

Roundabout driving school (history again!) to the rescue! It improved driver performance and may also represent economic opportunity.

Millions of people world-wide could be in need of roundabout training. Kenora has the expertise!

Opportunity knocks but once. How about promoting Kenora as an international centre of excellence for roundabout studies? I can see the sign at the entrance to the city: "Visit Kenora— Home of the 1907 Stanley Cup Champions and world renowned Roundabout School.

Summer residents probably knew nothing about it until they rolled into town last summer. Most instantly figured it out and sailed right through without a dented fender or rude finger wave until they bumped into the Big Spruce and got tangled up in its branches. Kenora's ultimate makeover looks great but street changes sometimes mean you can't get there from here. Not without another round in the roundabout, anyway.

Honey, I Super-Sized the Kids!

For the first time ever, overweight people outnumber average people in America. Doesn't that make overweight the average then? Last month you were fat, now you're average—hey, let's get a pizza! –Jay Leno

Honey, I shrank the kids! Times have changed. That 1970 movie deserves a sequel called Honey, I Super-Sized the Kids! But it's not just the kids. North Americans of all ages are super-sizing themselves but many are resisting with a multitude of diets.

The most popular weapon in the battle of the bulge is the Atkins diet which has many pros and constipations. Atkins is the talk of the town with people chewing the fat about eschewing carbohydrates. No carbs used to mean your car had fuel injection but now it refers to fuel ingestion by Atkins fans.

There are also many lesser known diets. These include the garlic diet that allows you to eat anything you want as long as you add loads of garlic. This diet comes with the slogan, "It's chic to reek." You don't necessarily lose any weight but you do look slimmer from a distance.

Then there's the beer diet, on which you can eat anything you want but you have to drink a case of Buttwider a day. You don't lose weight but you forget about your weight problems. There's also the one-month diet that guarantees you'll lose thirty days.

Whatever their differences, all diets have one thing in common: the second week is usually a lot easier than the first. By then you're probably off it.

Most diets provide lots of deprivation. No carbs on this one, no fat on that one, mostly grapefruit on another. "If it tastes good, spit it out," orders yet another. Dieters' bodies fight back with irresistible cravings. Any lost weight is usually regained along with a bit extra. This leads to yet another diet with often with the same result. It's the dreaded yo-yo diet phenomenon that leaves the hapless dieter more gravitationally challenged at the end of each cycle. Dieters vying for the no-belly prize end up getting thoroughly waisted.

Fad diets are a growth industry. Most dieters pile on the pounds as bank accounts of diet book authors grow fatter. The diet industry piles up the profit on overpriced special foods. After a few weeks on some regimes a person could be hundreds of dollars lighter.

In addition to actual diets, there are weight loss strategies such as rigging your fridge to make an oink sound every time you open the door. That might work for some but it might make others head out to rib night.

It seems there's a conspiracy theory about everything these days. My own conspiracy theory is that skilled cooks prepare and serve huge portions of diabolically tasty food in order to fatten everyone around them. This makes them look thinner. Good plan! If you really want to look slim, lose the diets. Just hang around with chubbier folks.

Stupidest Things Ever Said

Only two things are infinite—the universe and human stupidity, and I'm not so sure about the universe. –Albert Einstein

"I believe in my cosmetics line. There are plenty of charities for the homeless. Isn't it time someone did something to help the homely?" This query, attributed to singer Dolly Parton, comes from a page of a calendar on my desk that is titled "The Three Hundred and Sixty-Six Stupidest Things Ever Said."

I have, with alarming frequency, said monumentally stupid things. Some gaffes still embarrass me when I remember them years later. Flipping through the calendar, I feared that quotes from my personal babblings would occupy a few dozen pages. I was relieved to find I wasn't quoted once! What's even more incredible, Canadian politicians, despite noteworthy accomplishments in the field, didn't get as much as an honourable mention.

The calendar was printed in the U.S, so perusing the calendar was like watching the Olympics on CNN. If Americans didn't win, it didn't happen. Naturally, Americans gave themselves credit for almost every achievement in the field of stupidity. That is their right, as George Bush made perfectly clear in one of his personal contributions: "American freedom is the example to which the world expires."

141

More inspired idiocy came from former Vice President Dan Quayle's prediction: "Whatever is going to happen is going to happen when it happens, regardless of what happens." With a blueprint like that, how can mankind fail to reach its destiny?

Canadian politicians do deserve recognition for their stupid utterances. Don Cherry could fill his own annual calendar. Jean Pelletier's reference to Olympic gold medalist Miriam Bedard as a pathetic single mother got him shot down from a plum patronage position, and further showcases the talent of Canadians. Chretien, as he did for George Bush, could have defended Pelletier with "He is a friend of mine. He isn't a moron at all."

Sponsorship money should flow through a Quebec advertising agency to fund a Canadian edition of "Stupidest Things Ever Said." It would increase our national pride and help keep Quebec in the fold! Since it's my idea, I should get a commission of several megabucks to maintain the glorious tradition of the sponsorship program.

On the other hand, maybe the Canadian calendar should list the 365 stupidest ways to spend tax dollars. The Auditor General has done the research already!

Jean Chretien's following statement proves the worthiness of Canadians in the field of stupidisms: "I don't know: a proof is a proof. What kind of a proof is a proof? A proof is a proof and when you have a good proof, it's because it's proven."

Chretien, despite obvious talent, was not particularly well-recognized on the world stage for saying stupid things. It could be because nobody could tell what he was saying. He demonstrated that with: "I cannot comment on something that I don't know. I have enough problem with the problem I know, so I don't want them that I don't know."

But why would people part with hard earned, after-tax dollars to buy a calendar with a colossal gaffe on each page? My theory is that lots of us gaffe so often that it is comforts us when others do, especially when they are prominent public figures. Misery loves company!

Tired, Retired and Re-Retired

My retirement from teaching last year left me with more time on my hands and less income in them. In order to fill the gaps, I did a few days of substitute teaching.

To qualify as a "supply," I needed a letter from the police verifying that I'm not a criminal. Fortunately, the investigating officer had never seen one of my lessons, and since I'd committed no other crimes, I soon had the letter in hand.

I abruptly found myself in a classroom full of adolescent boys with sperm-dimmed eyes competing loudly for the attention of girls who were fully absorbed in giggling their way to academic excellence. I had to establish control.

"No problem," I thought. "Here's where all that experience pays off." Every teacher who survives to retirement has developed their own strategies to maintain order in the classroom. Personally, I had honed the soporific qualities of my lessons to the degree that I had merely to capture the attention of students for a few microseconds and they would be fast asleep. That model behaviour would persist until it was rudely interrupted by the bell at the end of the period. This technique worked smoothly and ensured harmonious relationships and a peaceful environment in which my lessons could proceed without interruption.

The realities of supply teaching came as a shock. The primary objective is to ensure that the school is still standing and that students are still alive and uninjured at the end of the day. As a supply teacher I didn't have enough authority to capture the students' attention, even for an instant. My time-tested technique of involuntary sleep induction failed miserably. Students were able to remain conscious for periods of time I'd never imagined possible. I had to resign myself to periods of riot control that seemed to last longer than the last ice age and during that, like Rodney Dangerfield, "I don't get no respect."

Laughter, the best medicine

"There ain't much fun in medicine, but there's heck of a lot of medicine in fun." –Josh Billings, *19th century humourist*

It's ten years since my first article in the *Enterprise*. I'd never written anything for publication before and had never intended to. Then along came the spectre of a dump one hilltop away from pristine Silver Lake. I couldn't resist.

Since then I have worked to strengthen my writing skills: pumping irony, lifting passages, dodging the issues, stretching the truth.

Lately, I have gotten more serious about it. It's a humour column, supposedly, in that the occasional person has actually laughed. Since laughter is reputed to be the best medicine, I decided I should join the health care professions and deliver more of those benefits.

Given the contribution of laughter to health, it would be nice if the Ministry of Health would cut me a cheque for my services. Since that's not likely, I have to be content with the most meaningful payment ... being told that someone enjoyed a particular column, or more satisfying, that they actually laughed out loud.

The government would also be wise to note that I have the solution to the health care funding crisis. As you probably know, the proportion of government revenues which goes to healthcare is rising. If this continues, health care will soon soak up so much of the budget that education will no longer be funded. At this point there will no longer be much training of health care professionals, so the cost of paying them will drop. The system's actually self-correcting if we simply keep throwing more money at it.

Cell Phone Crackdown

It's going to be different in cottage county this year now that the Ontario government has started to combat the carnage caused by weapons of mass distraction. In an impressive display of legislative efficiency, Queen's Park passed a law banning the use of hand-held cell phones while driving. For those who find governments slow to act, this was reassuring proof that our legislature can address problems with breathtaking speed in a pinch. In a mere eleven years, without a single perogy (prorogue) break, from its first introduction as a private member's bill, the government of Ontario was able to pass the new law.

Too bad they got it wrong. Research has shown that people can't even walk safely, much less drive, while talking on a cell phone. A recent experiment showed that people talking on a cell phone were only half as likely to notice a polka dot-suited, red-nosed clown on a unicycle riding circles around them compared to others who were simply listening to music or engaged in conversation.

It doesn't make much difference whether the phone is hands-free or hand-held. It appears to be the preoccupation of conversing on the phone which makes a driver as dangerous as being drunk. The brain, apparently, is what does the real driving. What would really improve safety is a heads-free cell phone. However, the driver's hands are the brain's vital accomplices so it's a step forward to have them freed for action, just in case the otherwise busy brain manages to sense danger.

Now that modern technology has freed the hands of cell phone users perhaps it can bring similar benefits to those burdened by the many multitasking demands of modern driving. Ways to increase road safety are limited only by our imagination. How about hands-free urine bottles for long-distance truckers on the go? What about a hands-free make-up kit, complete with hands-free eyebrow plucker and hair brush for the cougar on the prowl? (Maybe they could be built into the phone. Don't they already come equipped with camera, waffle-iron, and hair dryer?) What about hands-free dog spankers to keep Fido out of the driver's lap?

Drivers are busy people, so many find it necessary to eat on the move. Hands-free steering wheel operation is achieved by keeping both thighs firmly on the wheel at the 8 and 4 o'clock positions. Still, a hands-free device for gnawing fried chicken while using your Bluetooth would be a safety breakthrough. It would ensure that the hands are free to drive and that the steering wheel remains free of the grease that can cause loss of steering control.

A device already exists that enables musicians to play guitars while annoying us with harmonicas. Perhaps it could be adapted for hands-free eating. Goodbye finger-lickin' good! Hello hands on the wheel, eyes on the road. But whither wanders the mind?

Cutting the Cheese Deemed Act of Terror

The officious lady at the airport security was clearly frustrated. It was already past eight in the morning and she hadn't confiscated anything all day. At least that's the best reason I can think of why she would have confiscated our cheese spreaders.

Cheese spreaders! Their pitiful blades might terrorize a tub of Philadelphia cream cheese, but certainly not the city. Their wooden handles were carved and painted to resemble pot-bellied, middle-aged people with oversized sunglasses and garish beach clothing. A hijack attempt with them might have rendered the crew helpless with laughter. Purchased as gag gifts, the cheese spreaders were intended to inflict mock damage on the egos of our pot-bellied middle-aged friends.

Supposedly disarmed, we continued to board the aeroplane with four bottles of duty-free wine in our carry-on bags.

Glass bottles! Glass bottles are easily broken to make awesome weapons. Winston Churchill recognized this during his very famous speech: "We shall fight on the beaches, we shall fight in the landing grounds, we shall fight in the fields and in the streets, we shall fight in the hills ... " During the uproar that followed those words of his 1940 speech, Churchill is reputed to have muttered to a colleague beside him, "and we'll fight them with the butt ends of broken beer

150

bottles because that's bloody well all we've got!'"
Wine bottles aren't always allowed, though.
In Whitehorse, the liquor store has a bottle-it-yourself section which has good wine at great prices. I loaded up on bargain goof and tried to take it to Yellowknife, where wine is priced as liquid gold.

The airport security agent ruled that the contents of the bottles were not allowed on board since they were not factory sealed. But for our archaic liquor laws, I would have done an on-the-spot product safety demonstration. Defeated, I handed the wine to the security person and told her to have a nice day. I'm sure she did.

For a while, even knitting needles were banned from commercial flights. Then came the revelation that knitting needles are usually carried by older ladies determined to finish baby booties during the plane ride to visit a new grandchild. Anyone who interferes with those plans may be terrorized by a raging granny. It was better to just let Granny knit.

Now, since a recent terrorist plot, all liquids and gels are banned on commercial flights. No more toothpaste, no more sunscreen, no more perfumes or deodorants and no more wine bottles in carry-on luggage.

The ban on liquids won't last. Big business wields a lot of power and passengers loading up on duty-free booze mean big bucks. A way to get wine and profits flying higher than ever will soon be found.

Ah-ha! I'm ahead of the wave! The previous

prediction was written only a few days ago and duty-free bottles are already flying high along with small containers of toiletries. Not only that, but my old practice of using zip-lock plastic bags as Gucci toiletry bags is now compulsory for all air travelers.

Cutting the cheese, however, may still be an act of terror.

In Praise of Pavlov

"Advertising may be described as the science of arresting the human intelligence long enough to get money from it." –Stephen Leacock

The bane of a dog owner's existence is doggie drool. (Doggie stool is high on the list too, but that's another issue). Every time food is likely to appear Rover drenches his surroundings with slobber.

Imagine devoting your life to making dogs drool! In his very famous experiment, Russian psychologist, Pavlov, did exactly that. By consistently ringing a bell just before feeding his dogs, he found that dogs would eventually salivate at the sound of the bell, whether or not food was presented. This became known as conditioned response.

You and I might be more interested in discovering a way to stop dogs from slobbering, but scientists are a different kind of cat.

Pavlov's findings have been applied by modern marketers, for whom consumers are the new droolers. Pavlov's bell has been replaced by advertising of great bargains, along with the promise of consumer's nirvana: blinding white teeth, silken tresses, six-pack abs. According to the ads all we have to do is buy the right beer and we will spend the rest of our perfect lives surrounded by our fellow beautiful, young and sexy people.

The words "SALE" or "SAVE" in big bold print, or screamed hysterically over the radio or TV induces the shopper's equivalent of dogs drooling. That's the uncontrollable urge to spread their cash in anticipation of gobbling up supposed bargains or getting one step closer to the perfect life.

The most common type of sale promotion is discounting. "Regular" prices are jacked sky high to permit huge discounts. Huge, often phoney, discounts cause shoppers to slobber cash right into the cash boxes of the nation.

Clearance sales are the bargain whore's opportunity for great bargains on discontinued stuff or end of season leftovers. There are huge savings on vile yellow plaid polyester bell-bottoms with 52 inch waists and 26 inch inseams ... even cheaper if you buy two pairs. Dedicated bargain hunters and their families have a distinctive appearance and are easily recognized. Consumers are also conditioned to drool wildly for special occasions like Valentine's Day, Halloween, Mother's Day, Father's Day. Slogans like "Shop like Santa, Slave like Stooge" urge us to wallow in junk.

As Stompin' Tom Connors used to sing it "we'll save a lot of money spendin' money we don't got." Keeps the economy healthy but may destroy the planet in the process. Actually, the planet will be fine. It's mankind and everything we value that's at risk. Perhaps our biggest need is to want less.

The Oenophile's Files

Wine is sunlight, held together by water. –Galileo Galilei

What has nice legs, great body, is a pleasure to the lips and delightful to the tongue? Hint: It's great all the way to the bottom, goes down easily and has a long, smooth finish.

Give up? The answer is Marilyn Merlot.

With ever more different wines on the shelves these days, it's hard for any particular winemaker to make sure that a bottle of their goof makes it into your shopping cart. Wacky names are the latest ploy by vintners to cajole you into selecting their product.

It's working! Informal polling of my friends showed that many had tasted Cat's Pee on a Gooseberry Bush and some have even soaked in the tub with a little Fat Bastard. Others have been hopped up on Arrogant Frog or French Rabbit. You've got to admit that names like those grab more attention than Bright's House Red.

Some other possibilities include Some Merlot of '42, Baco Noir to the Future, Don Chianti and Chateau l'over la Place.

With red wine having attained health food status, more and more amateurs are drinking wine. To help them make informed wine choices, aspiring connoisseurs can upgrade their skills by taking wine-tasting classes. What's next? Degrees in burger tasting?

Most of us crave variety but choosing a

different bottle of wine from the shelves is always a crap shoot. For help with your choice you might consult with friends or ask the gaggle of oenophiles begging change near the liquor store. As to the best buy, most of us just take a wild stab based on whim, price, and the bafflegab on the label.

Our desire for variety is illustrated in a joke about the nun who was overjoyed to hear Mother Superior announce that there was a case of gonorrhea in the convent. "Thank God," she said, "I'm so tired of chardonnay."

If conscience prods you to buy Canadian, you'll find many good Canadian wines on the shelves. Years ago our home-grown wines were abysmal, but many felt that if Canadian winemakers got enough practice, they would improve. Thanks in part to the persistent efforts of true patriots, myself included, who managed to choke down countless gallons of vile goof like Gimli Goose and Baby Duck, Canadian wines have steadily gotten better.

My normal choice of wines is home-made plonk, considered well-aged if it has been bottled already. Anything bottled over a month is vintage.

Imagine my excitement when I recently had the privilege of savouring some Château Trotanoy 1995. French red. Eleven years old! $400 bucks a bottle. Wonderful stuff, but it was the price tag and the following gushing description of the wine's mystical properties made a lasting impression on this guzzler.

"The 1995 boasts a saturated deep purple colour, followed by a knockout nose of black truffles, cherries, raspberries, and kirsch fruit intermixed with spicy oak and beef blood-like scents. Full-bodied, dense, and as powerful, this broad-shouldered, super-extract boasts long, sweet fruit and a caressing texture marks the finish."

That's not a bottle. It's a crock! Up your glass!

April Fools!

The following piece was an April Fools spoof that I had written back in 2009. Just as I was ready to send it to the Lake of the Woods Enterprise for publication, the publisher called me in to his office and fired me. Well, he didn't really fire me; he just told me that he couldn't pay me for any more articles because the mother corp was cutting off the budget for local freelancers. Mother Corp had got in financial trouble in the big crash of 2008 and was milking the profitable papers by canning local writers and substituting locally irrelevant and cheaper content from outside sources. I wasn't into toiling away to enrich the Mother Corp shareholders so "Lateral Thinking" died.

Since I had an article ready the publisher agreed to make an exception for that one piece. I submitted it, they printed it, and I billed them for it. The cheque never came. I re-billed and they still never paid. It turned out that they also had a policy of not paying any accounts under $100. Catch 22, sort of. They couldn't pay me because they didn't owe me enough (rule #2) and they would never owe me enough because of rule #1. Diabolically clever! I could have chased them for it or re-billed a higher amount but the irony was priceless. Getting stiffed for an April Fools piece! How do you beat that? On the bright side, I may have been the fool, but not fool enough to ruin a story like that over a few bucks! There! I finally *got to print the story behind the story.*

Worldwide Threat from Dangerous Chemical

Regular readers of *Lateral Thinking* may be taken aback by the serious nature of this article. I have always written about topics which could provide a bit of a chuckle. Not this time. I'll be wearing my tree-hugger hat instead of the usual wanna-be-funny chapeau.

We've been living with a potentially devastating environmental threat that has been present for some time, and I feel it is my duty to bring it to public attention. A chemical known as DHMO is already widely spread in our area.

DHMO, di-hydrogen monoxide, is a colourless and odourless chemical that kills thousands of people each year, usually through accidental inhalation. Under certain conditions it may cause severe burns and has been found in the tumours of cancer patients.

In addition to the devastating health consequences, this chemical is a major factor in the erosion of our landscape. It accelerates the corrosion of metals and is often a cause of electrical failures and the decreased effectiveness of automotive brakes and steering, leading to many fatalities. Financial losses due to DHMO, especially in tsunamis and hurricanes have already been catastrophic and many have been affected by it worldwide.

Despite the dangers of DHMO it's widely used as a fire retardant, as an industrial solvent, and as a coolant in nuclear power plants. It's present in our food and no amount of washing will remove it.

In spite of the evidence against it, governments are steadfast in their refusal to limit the production, distribution and use of this chemical. This lack of action may be due to resistance from private interests, huge corporations and economists who fear that a ban on DHMO may produce disastrous results.

Their claims include potential damage to public health and world economies.

Earth Day presents a special opportunity for citizen action against environmental threats like DHMO, including discussion of how we can bring this threat to public attention and spur political action.

Those of you with even the slightest smattering of high school chemistry still trapped in your noggin probably recognized the April Fool spoof right off the hop. Decoding the chemical nomenclature reduces DHMO to H_2O which everybody recognizes as water.

Talking Trash

Until relatively recently there were small landfills scattered around the countryside. Initially, these were free to use and unsupervised. Later they came under management and finally they were closed altogether and replaced by one large landfill site which is engineered to higher standards and less likely to pollute.

Laclu Shopping Centre

Feeling down in the dumps? Maybe a shopping trip is what you need to lift your spirits. Try an excursion to a one-stop shopping centre that has almost every type of consumer item known to man and where any trade is accepted. In this consumer paradise whatever you take is free, but you pay to drop off your junk.

I'm referring to the Laclu Shopping Centre. Some may call it the Laclu Dump but it's a sanitary landfill site to the truly genteel. I'm not sure why the land needs filling but that's another issue.

Anyway, the Laclu Dump is setting a new standard in shopping convenience. Never mind free parking. You don't even have to park! Drive-thru shopping convenience has arrived. Peak shopping times follow the long weekends when the big shipments arrive. Sure, not all merchandise is in premium condition, but that's just the perfect challenge for disciples of the Red

Green School of Repair.

I was at that shopping centre a while back, restocking their displays with a selection of treasures from my garage. While there, I cruised around looking for some useful items to restock my garage shelves. As in regular stores, merchandise is frequently re-organized to encourage shoppers to look around more and make more impulse acquisitions. I browsed through the toy department, the recreational section and the home renovations section. Up until recently I'd always held the food department in very low esteem ... snobbishly turned up my nose at it, in fact. That attitude has changed.

People at the site are famished after their efforts at loading and unloading their trash. A steady stream of hungry customers arrive at the site, wallets at the ready. Location, location, location! The landfill's manager has recognized the unique potential of the site and operates a sideline business. He stocks a fine selection of ethnic foods in the cab of his truck and you can choose from home-made meat pies, perogies and cabbage rolls. We took advantage of this shopping opportunity and went away with a selection of food.

Meanwhile, my radio was tuned to Swap 'n Shop and I heard a voice advertising stuff for sale. Sounded like the stuff on my trailer. I looked in the mirror and spotted a guy on a cell phone lip-synched to the radio. I have for sale a lovely floor lamp and a dozen pieces of decking. Actually this event happened in my imagination, but it's a business opportunity with low start-up costs for someone.

On the way home, we stopped at Sal Vager's (real name withheld) place for a surprise visit. It was about lunch time. He had no quick lunch available so we provided our fine contribution of the recently-acquired dump delectable, which he was able to supplement with a side dish of road-kill rabbit.

Happily, the solid waste transfer station being built to serve the city will have a shopping centre ... an area where good junk can be put up for adoption by those who can use it (or at least store it for a while before putting it back into the cycle). It's an environmentalist's dream come true. Re-use is more environmentally sound than recycling. Now ... if they can only get a perogy shop into the plans!

Tales from the Dump

Stuffocation: being overwhelmed by the stuff one has bought or accumulated. –*Author Unknown*

I've been to Yellowknife a number of times and think it's a great little city. While there, I've enjoyed many of its typical tourist activities. I hung out with bush pilots. I got de-ranged at the Range, a lively bar where gamblers and prostitutes used to mine the miners. I practiced my lies in their parliament buildings. I toured historic Old Town and savoured the sweet sight of the antique honey-wagon as the shiny modern one sipped fresh nectar near-by. I chilled out at the Frostbyte Cafe, while marveling at the creativity of that name for a northern internet cafe. I visited the shanty-town with its unique street names like Ragged Ass Road. To get a true sense of the city, I read the local newspaper regularly, including a column called *Tales from the Dump*.

It seemed only appropriate to visit a facility that inspires the writing of a weekly newspaper column so I ventured beyond the usual tourist haunts and found myself admiring Yellowknife's alternative shopping centre and wildlife viewing centre. At the entrance, I was welcomed by the smiling, helpful greeter who was delighted to encounter a tourist. Following his instructions, I drove directly to the shopping experience I was looking for.

Stretched out before me was a vast open-air mall where a steady stream of delivery vehicles disgorged toys, furniture, clothing, electronics and sporting goods. It was as if Crawl-Mart, Slop-Easy, Extra Goods and Toys-R-Rust joined forces to redefine the shopping experience. Drive-in shopping at its finest!

I was at the dump, of course, although it's a sanitary landfill to the politically correct. Anyway, why was the land being filled? Was it empty?

Yellowknife dump is famous. I'd read about it in one of our national newspapers and heard about it on CBC radio. It's well known because scrounging is still allowed and encouraged. It's also renowned for the richness of deposits resulting from a highly transient population and the high cost of moving stuff out of the North.

Like ants at a picnic, scroungers prospected for treasure and filled their trucks, stopping occasionally to talk trash and conduct business deals. Good dumpmanship and camaraderie prevailed. There was no pushing and shoving as the claims were mined. Bargain hunters who found valuables they didn't want set them up on display for others. Shovelry is not dead.

I've studied dumpology. Despite nearly obtaining my PhD (like BS, only it's piled higher and deeper), I was unable to tell if scroungers were motivated by need, greed or love of the deed. They could have been simply saving a buck. They could have been business maggots collecting goodies for their next garage sale. Some could have been tree-huggers trying to save the planet. Double savings reward the avid scrounger: environmental and financial!

Yellowknifers had to fight hard to preserve this value-added endeavour. Kenoraites gave up almost without a fight. We've lost the right to free scrounge and all those great re-usables are denied a second career.

We no longer have a dump, just a transfer station. It's a savage blow to the ancient human tradition of living off the land. However, dump scrounging lives on for wildlife, although it's drastically down-sized. For ravens, seagulls and bears the transfer station is like Pizza Hunt or Eatin's. Wildlife is taking the won ton challenge. Rick Mercer would be thrilled.

Adventure Tourism Comes to Town

For some it's bungee jumping. For others it's sky-diving, white-water rafting, wild rides at an amusement park or even a trip over Niagara Falls in a barrel. Not me! I walk along Kenora's Railway Street. It's a world class adventure experience that works into my daily routine! This easy alternative is viable year round due to the narrow road and the fast, heavy traffic.

Especially in the winter, a walk along Railway Street is a death-defying experience. Adventure conditions are at their optimum! Picture it in your mind: The road is slippery, narrow and shrouded in exhaust fumes.

Banks of snow are piled high on both sides of the road. Luckily, much of the road has no shoulders, adding to your peril. You are walking along, your senses honed to their finest! Cars are hurtling by you in both directions along the icy roadway. Your mind races! "What if they don't see you? What if they skid? Could you jump out of the way in time? Could you clear the snowbank?" Your life hangs in the balance! Smugly, you realize that the faint of heart never travel this route.

Of course, this is nonsense! We obviously don't have a brilliant economic future based on adventure trekking on dangerous streets. But we do have quite a few places that are exceptionally hazardous to walkers, joggers and cyclists. Our citizens want and deserve streets that are safe for all users, especially children. It's possible to have them if we have the collective will to make the necessary improvements and shoulder the financial burden.

Adventure Starts Here!

As you drive into Kenora you are greeted by signs announcing "Adventure Starts Here." Elect a council that keeps that dream alive!

Promotion of extreme sports and adventure tourism should be a priority of any aspiring councilor. Sports like extreme skiing, mountain bike racing down cliffs, bungee jumping and waterfall kayaking are the rage these days. People pay big bucks for a high quality adventure experience. In order to vote intelligently, we should know what candidates would do to develop attractions for extreme sports enthusiasts and adventure tourists.

Key members of the present council have a very solid record on many issues like the wellness centre, attracting new industry, improved recycling and a number of other projects. However, their record on improving opportunities for adventure tourism within the city has been spotty. In one case the city actually ruined a major attraction. Main Street used to be a prime site for extreme jaywalking. Prior to last fall, adventure jaywalkers could zip out from behind a parked car and dart across four lanes of traffic in an act of death-defying, adrenalin-pumping, heart-thumping bravado. No more! With a few strokes of a paintbrush, jaywalking on Main Street, with its new island of safety in the centre, has gone from a thrill-seeker's dream to a haven of safety for sleepwalkers.

No wonder the change has been so controversial!

Be sure to ask candidates if they would act decisively and restore danger to Main Street.

Council, on the other hand, has enhanced some adventure tourism opportunities. Rabbit Lake Road used to be suited only to people interested in a nice peaceful stroll, jog, or bike ride. Drivers avoided the route altogether or moved slowly along the narrow band of rough terrain which was jokingly referred to as a road.

Now the band of bumps has been replaced by a ribbon of smooth, new pavement. Thankfully, the pavement was not made wider and no sidewalks or bikeways were provided. The resulting speedy traffic on the narrow roadway restores the adventure for self-propelled travelers. Adventure cyclists are especially well served by the changes to Rabbit Lake Road. The shoulders of a road are the normal escape for cyclists who chicken out and abandon the road in cowardly preference to becoming a hood ornament. However, the shoulders of Rabbit Lake Road are carefully crafted to enhance the adventure experience. A cyclist bailing out onto the shoulder might well find himself launched into space by giant moguls, bumper-stuffed into a mailbox, or rocketing down a steep embankment for a cool plunge in the lake. Literally, this is life on the edge! Good work, Kenora! We have the best of all worlds: Free adventure for locals and a tourist attraction combined!

Railway Street remains the best urban adventure experience in the city for the self-propelled thrill-seeker. The city has, in recognition of the need for adventure tourism attractions, acted proactively by not providing any sidewalks or bikeways on one of our busiest routes. Better yet, the shoulders of the road, where they exist at all, have all sorts of nifty adventure-promoting features. A cyclist may suddenly become airborne when the shoulder unexpectedly disappears into space or when their front wheel drops into a chasm. Utility poles lurk at the roadside to ambush the unwary cyclist in a manner worthy of Wiley Coyote. Electing a bunch of do-gooders to council will cause the degradation of this adventure paradise.

Promote the adventure experience. Vote for candidates who won't waste taxpayer's dollars on safety frills for a few fitness freaks who insist on walking, jogging or cycling in a world that is intended for the automobile.

On The Roads Again

Well, how about that? The snow came back again with a vengeance. Winter's like the axe murderer in a horror movie. You think he's gone and you're just starting to relax and all of a sudden, right out of the blue, he's back again, whacking someone else. They pinned the blame on the Alberta Clipper this time. Just like Alberta, too ... wishing for us Eastern bastards to freeze in the dark and then sending us the mechanism.

I'm not complaining about the white stuff. The ski season appeared to be over before the snowstorms came, but the snow put the trails back in top shape. I was returning from the ski club, travelling along Railway Street, noticing the high banks of snow piled up on both sides of the road. It looked like a snowboarder's half-pipe in places, with the steep snow piles right at the edge of the road on both sides. It was an adrenalin-seekers dream come true. Adventure in the making!

Adventure tourism is a big industry, but Kenora isn't blessed with the steep slopes and high snowfall that attract tourists to play in the avalanches. Nor do we have any deep chasms into which people can jump with elastic bands tied around their ankles. We lack raging rivers with huge whirlpools and long rapids for downhill kayaking. We have to make the best of our meagre resources.

The industry is still suffering from the taming

of Main Street. One of our few adventure tourism opportunities has been lost. The centre of the street, where traffic used to rush by on both sides of stranded jaywalkers, providing much sought after thrills, is now an island of safety. In the same fashion thrill-seekers would go to Pamplona to run with the bulls, they could flock to Kenora for extreme jaywalking with the locals.

Tourists and locals, cheated of one adventure experience, must now walk along Railway Avenue for the opportunity to flirt with death.

I was delighted to see that snow had restored optimum hazardous conditions to the ribbon of death. I expected to see a crowd of devil-may-care, risk tolerant, bullet-proof young men taking advantage of the danger. Imagine my surprise when I saw a woman clinging to the side of a steep snowbank in order to avoid sliding into the traffic. She had a young child with her!

I instinctively identified her as a graduate of the Steve Irwin and Michael Jackson School of Parenting. Instead of hanging her child over a balcony or dangling it a few inches away from the snapping jaws of a hungry crocodile, she was walking down Railway Street, toddler in tow. I expected to see the wild-eyed look of glee of a bungee jumper in mid-flight, but the expression on her face was that of sheer terror. Then the truth hit me. She was walking that hazardous stretch of roadway because she had to ... and she was terrified.

It's time that Kenora addressed the safety

problems that exist for walkers, cyclists, and motorists along the entire length of railway street, even if it will mean the end of adventure as we presently endure it.

Banking on Snowbanks

I was delighted recently to see that the snow that had fallen a week earlier was still piled along the sides of city streets. In many communities, much of that snow would have been thoughtlessly hauled away within hours. Some excellent opportunities would have been squandered.

Leaving the snow piled along the street curbs is a very wise and well-considered practice, especially along the busier downtown streets.

Consider the economic reality. We could be banking up the savings along with the snow. If the snow were hauled away just before one of those January heat waves that are so common every hundred years or so, it would be our hard-earned tax dollars that went down the drain, instead of a torrent of melt water.

As well, climbing over the snowbanks benefits many people who would not normally get much exercise. A minute scaling snowbanks is probably worth five on the treadmill and not everyone has a treadmill. Sure, the odd person might fall off a snowbank and crack their noggin or have a heart attack while tunneling to a parking meter. Some people might avoid going downtown to shop but those would be minor annoyances compared with the health benefits of a more physically fit population.

It's particularly comforting to see seniors rising to the challenge of scaling snow piles higher than mountains of broken election promises.

However, I don't think enough thought went into the decision to pile the snow along the curbs as opposed to piling it in the middle of the streets. For example, piling snow along the centre of Main Street would eliminate the problem of snow obscuring the yellow lines that mark the median. Snow piled on the median would clearly establish its presence and simultaneously restore the potential for adventure jaywalking. In an earlier article I lamented that the median strip on Main Street had created an unwelcome island of safety which had destroyed an opportunity for adventure tourism. Imagine the thrill of jaywalking across Main Street in rush minute if a huge mountain of snow were piled in the middle of the street. This would be a far more effective use of snow than piling it along the curb!

Brewed Awakenings are for the Birds

There are few pleasures equal to drinking in the incredible beauty of our natural world. Nowhere is that beauty more enjoyable than at the lake, especially when you are savouring the view of the lake and forest with a delicious cup of coffee in your hand. The background music that adds to the magic of this delightful experience is provided by nature herself. The air is filled with the beautiful sound of birdsong … or at least it should be. Sadly, with every year that goes by, that birdsong is diminished from the year before. Your choice of coffee can make a difference. Wake up and help to save our birds.

Many of the birds whose songs and beauty so enhance that wonderful summer experience are neotropical migratories. They come here in breeding season but the remainder of their year is spent in the tropics or in transit. Their continued survival is dependent on the existence of quality habitat here, in the tropics and at sufficient locations in between where they can rest and refuel during their long migration.

These avian seasonal residents are an essential component of our ecosystem, therefore ensuring their survival is a critical part of stewardship of our environment. That means we must try to ensure that bird habitat is protected in the faraway tropical wintering areas of Central and South America

As more and more land in those tropical areas

is converted from forest to agriculture, there's less and less winter habitat for forest-dwelling migratory birds. Much of the remaining habitat is provided by traditional coffee farms.

Traditional coffee farms consist of an understory of coffee bushes, a middle layer of fruit trees, and a canopy of tall hardwoods. These plantations provide excellent bird habitat for wintering songbirds, as well as local non-migratory bird species. Coffee grown in this type of plantation is rightly referred to as shade-grown, or simply shade coffee.

A few decades ago, the only known coffee was Arabica, which could only be grown in a shaded environment. Since then, strains of Arabica which will grow in full sun have been developed. Also, another species of coffee, Robusta, which requires full sun, was discovered. Because of these recent changes in coffee production, shade coffee plantations are a threatened habitat. A lot of coffee is now grown with no shade canopy at all. These modernized or "sun" coffee plantations result in a drastic decline in the diversity and number of birds that the plantation will support. Demand for shade coffee helps to ensure the survival of shade coffee farms and the habitat they provide. When the coffee in your cup comes from this type of coffee farm you're helping to preserve our wonderful natural world even as you are drinking it all in. The discovery that the right choice of your morning wake-up can help protect such a valuable part of nature may qualify as a brewed awakening.

You will pay a premium for your shade coffee but will be rewarded by the great flavour and the feeling that you're doing the right thing. However, you'll want to make sure that it really is beneficial to birds. It's difficult as a consumer to ensure that you aren't being ripped off as there's no established set of standards, nor an established certification body for shade, or bird-friendly coffee. That makes it tricky to make sure your coffee purchases support our feathered friends. One possibility is to locate coffee from trustworthy coffee roasters who buy raw coffee beans which are grown in a bird-friendly manner. You need to be sure that they are as diligent as possible in sourcing coffee from farms which really do preserve good bird habitat.

There are different classifications of coffee that relate to their stewardship of songbird habitat. These include "bird-friendly," "shade-grown" and "organic." Buying the right coffee might require some research to determine which available coffees will benefit migratory songbirds.

I have toured a number of coffee farms as an ecotourist and am totally sold on the shade concept. Shade-grown coffee plantations can, and usually do, provide habitat for all types of wildlife, especially birds.

However, the quality of a shade-coffee

environment can fall in the range from nearly indistinguishable from natural tropical forest to rather poor habitat with only a token amount of overstory. When choosing coffee, it can be difficult to know where the green stops and the greenwashing begins. There are no easy answers but the search for a good answer, and a good coffee, can be rewarding in itself. The Audubon Society and the Smithsonian Institute have a wealth of useful information on their websites.

In choosing your coffee, it's also worth noting that organic coffee is usually shade coffee. It's difficult to grow coffee organically without shade trees. Shade trees protect the understory coffee plants from rain and sun, help maintain soil quality, reduce the need for weeding and aid in pest control by providing habitat for birds. Organic matter from the shade trees also provides a natural mulch, which reduces the need for chemical fertilizers, reduces erosion and contributes nutrients to the soil.

Drinking the right coffee can be part of living greener and leaves a good taste in your mouth. Keep our feathered friends coming back and keep our environment healthy. Make sure your coffee is for the birds!

Vote Tory

Many Canadians are thinking of voting for the Tories but which party is that? The Conservative Party of Canada is using tory blue and some newspapers are calling them Tories. But are they?

The word "tory" comes from Irish roots and has been used since the 17th century. Tory evolved from "toraidhe" which meant "pursuer" and originally referred to highway robbers in the 1600s. Hang on! That sure sounds like the Liberals!

Years ago, the Reform Party was formed by disgruntled Conservatives who separated because they didn't want to be Tories. A few years later, they tried to wed the Progressive Conservatives to form the united right.

The resulting Canadian Conservative Reform Alliance Party (CCRAP pronounced see crap or c-crap with a stutter) was born. Before the laughter subsided, Reform shifted to the left and the "new" party became the Canadian Conservative Reform Alliance. That marriage failed when very few Tories jumped into the bed. The Alliance was just Reform with a new name.

A few years later, the Alliance wooed the PCs again, and finally won their hand in a shotgun marriage. The wedding was anything but gay, perhaps even anti-gay, with many of the PCs stomping out, stating reasons why the parties should not be joined. The ceremony was completed anyway.

The newlyweds became the Conservative Party of Canada, having removed the Progressive from Conservative. Judging by some of their policies, such as Reaganomics, they may well be the Regressive Conservatives, but are they Tories?

Given their origin, if they are Tories at all, they must be Reformatories. Or, if they really get to the bottom of things and expose the crap in Ottawa, their role will have been more suppository. More likely, if Stephen Harper continues with the soporific campaign ads and speeches, we'll know them as Dormitories.

The Reform Jonah may have swallowed the PC whale, but, perhaps due to digestive problems, there were enough leftovers to form yet another conservative party. Unable to use the name Progressive Conservative, they are running candidates in the election under the banner of the Progressive Canadians. Maybe they are the real Tories!

Whatever you call them, that Tory blue Trojan horse trying to sneak through the gates of Parliament is full of Reformers.

My Deep Political Slumber Had to End

Comedy is simply a funny way of being serious. –Peter Ustinov

I guess that I always used to trust governments to do the right thing. At least that's the excuse I'll use for being quite uninvolved in politics during the early part of my adult life. Sure, there were other factors. I was busy doing things of more concern or apparent benefit, but basically I was happy, or at least not desperately unhappy, about what was happening in the political sphere. That probably shows that I just wasn't paying enough attention.

Enter Stephen Harper and my Rip Van Winkle wake-up moment. I thought him to be an egomaniacal, confrontational control freak with few competent colleagues. Together, they disregarded evidence and expert opinion in their decisions. Instead, they ploughed ahead with an ideological agenda, dispensing favours to specific voter blocks to solidify their support with those groups, even when the overall impact on the country would be negative. The object was simply to carve off enough blocks of voter support (divide and conquer) to ensure reelection.

Combine the above with hyper-partisan advertising on the public dime, a spate of appointments of nefarious characters to high public office and firing of various public watchdogs who were doing their jobs too well.

The list could go on and on. The man, his party and their barrage of affronts have awakened me from my political slumber.

The final straw was the defunding of the Experimental Lakes Area (ELA) which was buried in an omnibus bill about the length of *War and Peace*

I was one member of a group which organized to make people aware of the ELA and the role it played in Canadian environmental science. I wrote the following open letter in 2012, about a year after the announced, impending closure of the ELA. It was published as an open letter in a number of newspapers. I felt that there was already enough serious commentary in the media without another dry article. Hence the following serious, *Lateral Thinking* style spoof that may have played some tiny part in the successful effort to ensure the survival of the Experimental Lakes Area research facility:

Harperocracy Tramples Democracy

That Stephen Harper and his gang, they're such kidders. Last May, when their Omnibus Bill defunded the Experimental Lakes Area research facility (ELA), everyone thought they meant to close it.

The world-renowned jewel, located near Kenora in Northwestern Ontario has for 44 years shown us how to best protect our lakes and rivers from acid rain, algal blooms, mercury pollution, and much more. ELA's research experiments on whole-lake ecosystems produce reliable results which enable governments to craft informed policies to minimize threats to our freshwater ecosystems.

Universities, environmental organizations, city and municipal councils, scientists, along with many members of the Canadian public missed the joke and were outraged at the closure. When intense pressure persisted, the government had to explain: "We were just goofin' around, that's all. We don't want to close ELA. We just want to find another operator."

The joke turned into an episodic comedy series when staff received layoff notices, researchers made other plans and the whole facility was thrown into disarray. What a Dilbert-worthy way to begin "searching diligently for another operator," as Environment Minister Peter Kent put it. Apparently, the best way to persuade someone to take over a successful operation is to wreck it first. Slapstick humour at its finest!

The government claims that the work at ELA, which shows how to protect freshwater fish habitat from the effects of human activity, doesn't fit the mandate of the Department of Fisheries and Oceans. Hilarious: fish habitat has nothing to do with fisheries! Great satire! With

185

logic like that it doesn't fit at Environment Canada, either. The Harper comedy team should write lines for 22 Minutes or Rick Mercer.

Though ELA costs each Canadian a paltry 6 cents per year, these straight-faced jesters claim that ELA is not cost-effective. ELA costs $2 million per year and has saved us billions in environmental damages and clean-up costs.

Closing ELA will cost up to $50 million ... the cost of operating ELA for the next 25 years! What a back-slapper! Clever self-satirization!

Malice in Blunderland could be responsible for the seemingly inexplicable, relentless attack on science. Could the closure of ELA be part of the dismantling of environmental protection to bulldoze a path for big oil?

Meanwhile, to add insult to idiocy, the Harper government spends millions on self-aggrandizing advertising which strangely fails to mention the F-35 fiasco or the end run around democracy with huge omnibus bills. Taxpayers are on the hook for thinly disguised election propaganda at many times the cost of operating ELA.

We are also going to shell out $5 million per year for the Office of Religious Freedom when our own scientists are not free to inform us, and we are not free to learn about their work. Good job, comedy team. Excellent irony!

To compound the hilarity, Kenora MP Greg Rickford plays "Where's Waldo?" as he refuses to attend public forums and ducks questions from constituents. He once couldn't say enough good things about ELA, but now, despite his billboards proclaiming that he's "a strong voice" for Northwestern Ontario, Mr. Rickford has no voice, strong or weak, to defend the impending closure. Perhaps the best defence is a good absence.

George Burns claimed that, in humour, timing is everything. Accordingly, if no white knight manages its rescue, Canada's world-renowned, unique research facility will be gone just in time for April Fools' Day. A fitting finale for a farce, perhaps. But not for the irreplaceable ELA.

Nonsense Revolution Carries Mountain to Mohammed

The latest inanity to emanate from the Common Sense, or is that Rotten Scents, Revolution is so ridiculous that it's a wonder that the Regressive Convertibles didn't do a cabinet shuffle just to make the announcement. The decision by the Ministry of Health to cut support payments to visiting specialists is worthy of John Snobelen. He made his mark in education with his skill at crises creation and in natural resources with his straight-faced about-face on the bear hunt. He was a shoo-in for the hat trick, the triple play of cabinet ministry.

Taken to its illogical conclusion, the decision to cut support funding for visiting specialists will result in their becoming visited specialists. They won't come here and Kenora patients in need of their services will go to them in Toronto, Thunder Bay, Winnipeg or wherever they happen to practice.

In this absurd modern day transport of the mountain to Mohammed we will have hundreds of patients scrambling for the money to fund trips to specialists. Since many are bound to be elderly patients or children with limited financial resources, considerable time, difficulty and sacrifice may be required to raise the money for transportation, lodging and food.

Some of that will be repaid later by the Northern Travel Allowance at immensely higher cost to the health care system than properly funding the visiting specialists in the first place. Nothing will compensate for the added stress and inconvenience. Common sense be damned! Revolution, maybe ... if you count circular logic.

To get another point of view, watch the government's slick ads about the tremendous strides that have been made by the Harass government in improving our health care system. You owe it to yourself to watch. You're paying.

Weren't we fortunate to have had those ads to comfort us during the stressful times when our hospital almost lost diabetic education, anesthesia and psychiatric services due to failure of the government to understand needs of the North? All this occurred while precious tax dollars bought ads to convince us that health care was improving.

Cynics might even conclude that the government is trying to buy our votes with our own dollars. Maybe if they cancel the ads, the millions saved would provide the thousands needed to cover support costs for the specialists. I'd have to do the math to be sure.

Sneaking Truth to Power

In response to the confusion, turmoil, criticism of management and the hospital board related to the hospital deficit triggered by a change in the government's funding formula for our local hospital, I wrote the following piece. It was intended to be humorous, but to also provide a quick, very superficial understanding of the model by which our hospital is funded. It was also intended to send the Ministry of Health a sledge-hammer subtle critique of why the funding model is failing and needs to be changed.

Hospital Funding De-Mystified

There are some things so serious that you have to laugh at them. –Niels Bohr

So, the hospital went a million smackers in the hole last year. The knee-jerk reaction would be to lay blame on the hospital board or administration, but if you dig into it a bit you might conclude that the people of the Kenora area and their guests were to blame.

Under the present model by which the province funds our hospital, the hospital gets part of its funding for doing specific treatments. For example, Lake of the Woods District Hospital (LWDH) historically has treated over a hundred cases of COPD (chronic obstructive pulmonary disease, in case you wondered) in an average year. Accordingly, the government funded the hospital for the treatment of 107 cases at 8 grand a pop. You might expect that with the financial health of the hospital at stake, sufficient number of eager residents would contract COPD and show up for treatment. Unfortunately, the citizenry failed in its duty last year. Too few showed with COPD and, as a result, roughly a quarter million was clawed out of the hospital coffers. The hospital had done its part. It remained on the ready for the usual influx, and, according to patient surveys, did a cracker-jack job of treating the dedicated patients who had the decency to show up. Similar clawbacks occurred because not enough people showed up with pneumonia, strokes, and other assorted ailments. In all, a half million dollars was clawed back because people failed to get sick in sufficient numbers and with the right ailments.

This component of the hospital funding has a somewhat Orwellian name. It is called QBP, for quality based procedures. Under this system, the more sick people treated, the higher the quality and efficiency are deemed to be, and the hospital is funded accordingly.

Visitors to Kenora also deserve a share of the blame. A good chunk of hospital revenue comes from treating patients from other provinces or counties. Part of the budget assumes that visitors will require their usual amount of hospital care. Last year our visitors neglected their duty to have sufficient car and boat crashes, illnesses and falls to meet the hospital's needs. Their anticipated contributions didn't arrive, thus contributing to the revenue shortfall.

In total, over a half million bucks was clawed back because too few showed up for specific treatments and another couple hundred thousand never arrived because tourists failed to do their part.

Looking at it another way, the bad news story of the hospital deficit was really a cleverly disguised good news story about residents and visitors being too healthy for the good of the hospital's revenue. Expenses, incidentally, came in right on budget.

If we're more fortunate next year, people will be sicker and the hospital will be in the black again. I didn't mean that. I was just goofin' around, that's all. Obviously the present funding model is a bit whacky. It doesn't work well for LWDH and it needs to change. Whaddya think?

Electoral Reform

*Democracy is the worst form of government
... except for all the others. –Winston Churchill*

Canada's electoral system is seriously flawed. In the last two elections majority governments were elected with less than 40% of the votes cast, giving them 100% of the power. More than 61% of Canadians' votes counted for nothing. Perhaps the best indicator of the flaws in our electoral system is the number of votes per MP elected: 37,000 per Liberal MP, 40,000 per Conservative, 111,000 votes to elect each NDP member, and a whopping 580,000 votes to elect a single Green Party MP.

In the last federal election campaign Justin Trudeau made a solemn, unequivocal promise that the 2015 election would be the last under the "first-past-the-post" (whatever that means), winner take all, electoral system. Since then a parliamentary committee with representation of all parties has consulted Canadians extensively and has heard overwhelmingly that Canada needs proportional representation and does not need a referendum for it to be implemented, but the committee then recommended a referendum on proportional representation.

The Liberal's action under Minister for Democratic Institutions, Maryam Monsef, has been to conduct an on-line survey, supposedly to gauge the desire of the public to change the electoral system. The survey contains no mention of changes to the electoral system and has been widely lampooned as some combination of con, scam and joke. Some questions appear biased in a way to make responders fearful of change. Other questions are loaded to evoke answers that favour the Liberal's pet form of voting reform, ranked ballots, that would significantly raise their chances of receiving even larger and more frequent majorities. That would make the system even more unfair.

So flawed is the survey that it has inspired a clever and hilarious spoof survey: MyDemocracy.con. To see it, google "take the globe's electoral reform survey." It's a riot!

You can find out more about electoral reform and take direct action on the internet sites **fairvote.ca** and **leadnow.ca**.

Canada's electoral system needs improvement and it's up to us to tell the government that we do want change.

What Do the Experts Say?

Use of quotations in conversation or writing is useful, helping the user to, perhaps fraudulently, appear knowledgeable, wise or witty. For that reason, I have long been a collector of both wise and witty quotations, sayings, quips and one-liners. What follows is a collection of my favourites.

"I'm writing a book. I've got the page numbers done." –Steven Wright

"I write what I know because that leaves me with a lot of free time." –Unknown

"I am a great believer in luck, and I find the harder I work the more I have of it."
–Stephen Leacock

"Not everything that can be counted counts, and not everything that counts can be counted."
–Albert Einstein

"The best argument against democracy is a five minute conversation with the average voter."
–Winston Churchill

"A kid prayed for a bicycle until he realized God doesn't work that way. So he stole one and asked for forgiveness." –Unknown

"It's hard to be religious when certain people are not struck by lightning."
–Calvin and Hobbes

"Men are from earth. Women are from earth. Deal with it." –George Carlin

"I have the greatest respect for everyone's religious obligations, no matter how comical."
–Herman Melville

"Religion gives people hope in a world torn apart by religion." –Jon Stewart

"Properly read, the Bible is the most potent force for atheism ever conceived."
–Isaac Asimov

"All dogs don't go to heaven; only the ones that have accepted Christ." –Colbert

"Reality is the leading cause of stress for those in touch with it." –Jane Wagner

"If you laid all the smokers end to end around the world 2/3 of them would drown."
–Unknown

"The problem with youth today is that I'm no longer part of it." –Unknown

"The word *aerobics* came into being when fitness instructors realized you couldn't charge $25 an hour for *jumping up and down*."
–Rita Rudner

"Memory is like a crazy old woman who hoards coloured rags and throws away food."
–Austin O'Malley

"Good health is the slowest rate at which you can die." –Unknown

"I intend to live forever. So far, so good." –Steven Wright

"You shouldn't eat dinners for four unless there are three other people." –Unknown

"Being a writer is like having homework every day for the rest of your life." –Lawrence Kasdan

"I don't know if God exists but it would be far better for his reputation if he didn't." –Jules Renard

"If God exists, I hope he has a good excuse." –Woody Allen

"Education is what remains after one has forgotten what one has learned in school." –Albert Einstein

"It's not an optical illusion. It just looks like one." –Unknown

"Everywhere is walking distance if you have the time." –Steven Wright

"I don't want to make the wrong mistake." –Yogi Berra

"If it weren't for my faults, I'd be perfect." –Unknown

"If you can't stand solitude, maybe you bore others, too." –Unknown

"It was snowing so hard when we took off that the pilot had to put chains on the propellers." –Unknown

"Pity the dyslexic agnostic insomniac who laid awake all night wondering if there was a dog." –Unknown

"I suffer from reincarnation anxiety. I'm afraid I'll come back as myself." –Unknown

"When you've heard one bagpipe tune, you've heard them both." –Unknown

"Never buy a pit bull from a one-armed man." –Unknown

"If your dog is fat, you aren't getting enough exercise." –Unknown

"The noblest dog is the hot dog. It feeds the hand that bites it." –Unknown

"Airline fees: A scrotum is soon to be classed as a carry-on bag." –Unknown

"We've got to take care of the environment. It's the only place we are still allowed to smoke." –22 Minutes

"Give a man a fish and he eats for a day. Teach him to fish and you get rid of him for the whole weekend." –Unknown

"I fish, therefore I lie." –Unknown

"I was wondering why the baseball was getting bigger. Then it hit me." -Stephen Wright

"If at first you don't succeed, forget skydiving." –Steven Wright

"Trying is the first step towards failure." –Homer Simpson

"The longest sentence you can form with two words is: 'I do.'" –HL Mencken

"A lot of hardened criminals resulted from a collision between a prison van and a concrete truck." –Unknown

"Honesty is the best policy but insanity is a better defence." –Steve Landesberg

"I don't feel like listening to any motivational speakers." –Unknown

"You won't hear opportunity knock if the TV is on." –Unknown

"War doesn't determine who's right, only who's left." –Unknown

"It's the greatest thing since they re-invented unsliced bread." –Unknown

"The universe is made up of electrons, protons, neutrons, and morons." –Unknown

"The cost of living is high but at least we get a free trip around the sun every year."
–Unknown

"Hardware is anything you can kick. software you can only curse at." –Unknown

"I almost had a psychic girlfriend but she left me before we met." –Steven Wright

"I looked up my family tree and found out that I was the sap." –Rodney Dangerfield

"People now take comedians seriously and politicians as a joke." –Will Rogers

"Trickle down economic theory: If you feed horse enough oats, some will pass through for the sparrows." –Unknown

"A fool and his money are soon elected."
–Will Rogers

"Politicians are like diapers. They should be changed often and for the same reason."
–Robin Williams

"We will all die someday if we live long enough." –Unknown

"Laughter is the shortest distance between two people." –Victor Borge

"The secret to a good sermon is to have a good beginning and a good ending and to have the two as close together as possible."
–George Burns

"He may look like an idiot and talk like an idiot but don't let that fool you. He really is an idiot." –Groucho Marx

"The fundamental freedoms are speech, assembly and superstition." –Unknown

"Those who have the privilege to know have the duty to act." –Albert Einstein

"Reality is the leading cause of stress for those in touch with it." –Jane Wagner

"Reality is a quest for those who can't take booze." –Unknown

"Of those who say nothing, few are silent." –Thomas Niell

"If ignorance is bliss, why aren't there more happy people?" –Philip Howard

"Being born beautiful is like being born rich and then getting steadily poorer." –Joan Collins

"Sobriety is great in moderation." –Unknown

"The word 'aerobics' came into being when fitness instructors realized you couldn't charge $25 an hour for 'jumping up and down.'" –Rita Rudner

"Time is nature's way of preventing everything from happening at once." –John Wheeler

"There is more to democracy than two wolves and a sheep voting on what to have for dinner." –James Bovard

Ponderings from a Confused Philosopher

How is it that almost everybody is an above-average driver?

Do some people get lost in thought because it's unfamiliar territory?

Isn't dogma a bitch?

Is it fruitless to eat vegetables?

Why is it that adolescence must end but immaturity can go on forever?

If an adolescent goes to jail, will their face break out?

Is it the crack of dawn that causes daybreak?

Can you back up down a hill?

Is poisoned soup dispacho?

Is a will a dead giveaway?

Does a backward poet write inverse?

How old would you be if you didn't know how old you were?

If you don't pay your exorcist can you get repossessed?

Has the guy who fell onto an upholstery machine been fully recovered?

If you don't join dangerous cults, are you practicing safe sects?

If you can't find the key, should you break into song?

Are bagpipes the missing link between music and noise?

Do marathon runners with bad shoes suffer the agony of de feet?

Has atheism always been a non-prophet

organization?

Why are there no lineups at the restroom of a public swimming pool?

Since 75% of heat loss is from your head, can you put on a good hat and ski naked?

Is real poo better than shampoo? Would you buy tires at a blow-out sale?

If a Canadian falls in the forest, will he apologize?

Lateral Thinking Comes to a Sorry End

We're a sorry lot, us Canadians. Masters of apology. It seems that no matter what happens, an apology is warranted. If you step on my foot, we both apologize. If I step on your foot, we both apologize. The propensity for apology is so deeply entrenched in the Canadian psyche that the Province of Ontario deemed it necessary to pass the Apology Act which states that an apology is not an admission of guilt. With this law in place, if you apologize for breaking someone's fist with your nose, the apology will not constitute admission that you are guilty of assault.

It seems you have read my book, so I owe you an apology. If you enjoyed the book I'm sorry that it wasn't longer and that your reading pleasure was inexcusably curtailed by its premature termination. If you didn't enjoy the book, I apologize for the imposition on your time. If my humour offended you in any way, of course I'm sorry about that. However, if you treasure offensive humour, and didn't find it, what can I do but apologize?

I'm sorry it had to end this way.